"You've got to prove it, Zane."

"Prove that I want you?" His hands gripped Caroline's hips and pulled her down harder against him. "I don't think there can be any doubt of that."

"Prove that you really think I'm strong. That you're not afraid I'll break at the least little thing."

"I know you won't."

"That you can still get lost in me. That we can get lost in each other."

Zane's hand reached up and tangled in her hair, bringing Caroline's lips down hard against his. Caroline moaned. *Yes*. Yes, this was what she wanted...

PROTECTOR'S INSTINCT

Janie Crouch

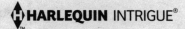

HARLEQUIN INTRIGUE®

This book is dedicated to Girl Tyler. It's wondrous to have a friend
who can walk with me through this craziness known as—duh, duh,
duh—writer's life. Thanks for all the talks, encouragement, TMI
shares and getting messages to me from editors when I'm out of
the country. And ALL CAPS. And All the Words. Boldly go, babe.

ISBN-13: 978-1-335-72140-2

Protector's Instinct

Copyright © 2017 by Janie Crouch

Recycling programs
for this product may
not exist in your area.

Printed in U.S.A.

Janie Crouch has loved to read romance her whole life. The award-winning author cut her teeth on Harlequin Romance novels as a preteen, then moved on to a passion for romantic suspense as an adult. Janie lives with her husband and four children overseas. She enjoys traveling, long-distance running, movie watching, knitting and adventure/obstacle racing. You can find out more about her at janiecrouch.com.

Books by Janie Crouch

Harlequin Intrigue

Omega Sector: Under Siege

Daddy Defender
Protector's Instinct

Omega Sector: Critical Response

Special Forces Savior
Fully Committed
Armored Attraction
Man of Action
Overwhelming Force
Battle Tested

Omega Sector

Infiltration
Countermeasures
Untraceable
Leverage

Primal Instinct

CAST OF CHARACTERS

Zane Wales—Former police detective in Corpus Christi, Texas, who has now become a pilot. His white hat is definitely retired since he can't trust his own judgment.

Caroline Gill—Corpus Christi paramedic who survived a brutal attack by a serial rapist eighteen months ago.

Tim Harris—Captain of the Corpus Christi Police Department and Caroline's close family friend.

Wade Ammons—Detective for the Corpus Christi Police Department.

Raymond Stone—Detective for the Corpus Christi Police Department.

Damien Freihof—Terrorist mastermind. Determined to bring down Omega Sector piece by piece by doing what they did to him: destroying their loved ones.

Mr. "Fawkes"—Omega Sector traitor providing inside information to Freihof.

Jon Hatton—Omega Sector Critical Response Division profiler who worked on a case eighteen months ago with Zane in Corpus Christi.

Lillian Muir—Omega Sector Critical Response Division SWAT team member.

Donald Brodey—Criminal whom Zane arrested when he first became a detective.

Omega Sector—A multiorganizational law enforcement task force made up of the best agents the country has to offer.

Chapter One

You're a liar. And everyone is going to know.

Caroline Gill glanced at the text on the phone, then promptly shut it down and put it away. She had ignored similar texts for the last four days, hoping they would stop. Someone obviously had the wrong number.

Caroline may be a lot of things, but a liar wasn't one of them. Life was too short to live surrounded by lies.

She'd learned that the hard way eighteen months ago.

She made a mental note to call the phone company or look into how to block texts on her phone after her shift tonight.

Because she definitely didn't have time to do it right now. She had a real crisis to deal with. As the ambulance pulled to a stop, Caroline jumped out of the passenger side and surveyed the utter chaos around her.

As she looked around the wreckage, she took a deep breath, trying to ascertain what she needed to do first. The thick morning fog that had blown in from the coast of Corpus Christi made everything more difficult to deal with—especially a deadly crash.

As a paramedic she dealt with accidents and injured people on a daily basis. Thankfully she didn't experience a situation as bad as this often: at least seven cars in a deadly pileup.

She turned back to her partner, who was just getting out of the ambulance. "Kimmie, radio Dispatch. We need help. Mass casualty. Let them know."

Kimmie did so immediately as Caroline further studied the situation before her. The fog had been a big factor in what caused this multicar pileup on State Highway 358. But a bigger factor looked to be like some idiot who had been driving the wrong way down the crowded street.

"Help me."

Caroline heard the weak voice coming from a truck a few yards away, just one of many. Some were sobbing, some begging for help, some basically screaming. Absolute chaos in a situation where no one could see more than two or three feet in front of them.

Caroline blocked out the voices—she had to, despite their volume or the words or sounds they made. She had learned a long time ago as a paramedic that the loudest people weren't always the ones who needed the most help.

Caroline pulled on gloves as Kimmie came running around from the driver's seat of the ambulance they'd arrived in together. "Dispatch is sending who they can. There's multiple calls because of this fog."

Caroline pulled out her triage kit, including the tags of four different colors inside. "We're going to have to tag everyone until help gets here. Thirty-second evaluations, okay? Green for minor injuries. Yellow for non-life-threatening. Red for life-threatening. And black…"

Caroline faded out. They both knew what black meant. Dead or so near to dead the victim couldn't be helped now.

Kimmie looked a little overwhelmed. Caroline's partner was relatively new and this was probably her first mass casualty situation. "Kimmie, you can do this. You've done it in training. Don't spend more than thirty seconds with each person and make sure the tag is the first thing seen when more help arrives."

They split up and began the always difficult job of choosing who would be treated first when more help arrived. Everyone was hurt. Everyone was scared. Everyone wanted to be the first ones treated. But they couldn't all be.

Caroline sprinted to the first victim, who unfortunately didn't take long to be evaluated. He was lying on the pavement covered in blood. He obviously hadn't been wearing his seat belt and the force of the impact had thrown him through the windshield. Caroline quickly searched for a pulse, felt none, so removed her hands before trying once more, hoping she was wrong. A lot of blood loss didn't always equate to death.

But in this case it did. "Damn it," she muttered under her breath before pulling out a black tag and placing it near the man's head. This would discourage other first responders from stopping for him until the other more critical cases could be taken care of.

She ran to the man screaming at the top of his lungs next. His car was the one facing the wrong direction. She braced herself for what she would find because of the sheer volume of the man's yells. But instead of finding some gaping wound or bones protruding in a hideous injury, she found a man, probably in his late twenties, holding his hand where it looked like his pinkie was dislocated.

"Thank God," he said as soon as she got close enough. "What took you soo-long?"

If the words slurring together didn't give her enough of a clue of his drunken state, the stench of alcohol that immediately accosted her senses did.

"Sir, are you injured besides your finger?"

"My finger is *broken*, not injured." He held it up as proof. "And the window of my car is smashed and the door won't open. I need you to fix that right away."

What did he think this was, AAA? Caroline didn't have time for this jackass who—coupled with the fog—had probably been the cause of this entire situation.

"Sir, I need to know if you have any more injuries.

There will be someone here soon who can help you get the door open."

The man just narrowed his eyes and let out a string of obscenities. "Don't you leave me here, you bitch."

Caroline could hear the cries of other people, including at least one child. She vaguely wondered if she smashed her elbow in this guy's face if it would look like something that just happened in the wreck. But she forced herself not to.

She handed him a yellow card. "Sir, give this to the next EMT or firefighter who comes your way, okay?"

The man immediately scoffed and threw it on the ground. "Don't you dare leave me. All these people were driving on the wrong side of the road." He grabbed her arm through the window. "I'll have your job if you leave me."

She grabbed his other, uninjured, pinkie, bending it back, knowing the pressure would cause him to release her arm. It was one of the self-defense moves she'd learned in the multiple classes she'd taken over the last year and a half.

No man would use his strength against her and make her a victim ever again.

"Unless you want me to break your other pinkie," she said to the drunk guy, "I suggest you let me go. Besides, you're going to be too busy sitting in jail to have my job."

The man released her and went back to yelling his obscenities at the top of his lungs. Caroline picked up the yellow tag and removed the adhesive cover on the back, sticking it to the outside of the car. Hopefully the guy wouldn't mess with it. She quickly moved on to the next car.

"Please help me." A mother was sobbing in the driver's seat, blood dripping from her face. A young girl and a baby sat in the back seat. The little girl was crying also.

"Ma'am, I'm here. It's okay," Caroline said, taking in the situation. The woman was pinned inside her vehicle where the front end had been crushed when it had been rear-ended into a safety railing. Her legs were trapped.

"My kids." The mom was hysterical, unable to see or help her children in the back. "Why is Nicole crying? Are they hurt? Is the baby okay?"

Caroline used her flashlight to shine into the car as she talked to the woman. "Hey, what's your name?" she asked the mom as she pulled on the door handle, but it wouldn't budge. The woman's legs were definitely pinned. The firefighters would have to get her out of here.

"Jackie."

Caroline couldn't tell what state Jackie's legs would be in, but for right now she was a yellow card. Needed help, but wasn't life-threatening. But the woman was still sobbing.

"Jackie, I'm going to check the kids now. But I need you to stop crying, okay? And hold this." She gave the woman the yellow tag. "This lets the firefighters know what to do."

She could see Jackie try to get herself under control. "My kids. Please, my kids."

Caroline touched her on the shoulder through the window that had been broken. "I'm checking right now."

She moved to the back door and opened it. A little girl in the back, about three years old, was sobbing, obviously terrified.

"Jackie, what's your daughter's name?"

"Nicole."

"Hey, Nicole," Caroline crooned. "You doing okay, sweetie?" The fog floating around the car and her mother's cries were frightening the girl. Caroline touched her gently on the cheek and she settled a little bit.

"I want Mama," the little girl said, hiccuping through her tears.

"I know you do. It will be just a few minutes, okay? Does anything hurt, sweetheart?" The girl seemed to be fine, but it was difficult to tell.

"No. I want Mama."

"I'm here, sweetie." Jackie was pulling herself together now that she could talk to her daughter. Nicole calmed down more as her mother did. "Is David okay?"

"Can you hold this for me, hon?" Caroline handed little Nicole a green tag. Someone else would check her out more thoroughly, but for right now, the girl didn't seem to need more medical attention. "Nicole seems fine, Jackie. I'm going to check on baby David now."

Baby David hadn't made a sound the whole time. Caroline's heart caught in her chest as she ran around the car to his side.

The baby, not older than six months, lay silently in his rear-facing car seat as Caroline pried open the door. As she reached over to check the baby's pulse, she could hear Jackie's ragged, terrified breathing.

She couldn't see any blood or noticeable injuries, but he didn't move at all at her touch. Caroline sent up a silent prayer that the child was alive. With babies, everything was tricky, since they were unable to communicate.

She found his pulse at the exact moment little David opened his eyes. He studied Caroline intently before taking his thumb and jamming it in his mouth, sucking on it.

"He's okay, Jackie. He's sucking his thumb." She reached over David and squeezed Jackie's shoulder. "I can't say for certain that he is injury free, but he's alive and he's alert." Caroline laid a yellow tag on baby David. He probably could be green-tagged, but with a baby she'd rather be safe than sorry. Someone would still need to check him more thoroughly.

"Jackie, you saved your kids' lives by having them properly restrained in their car seats. You did great. I have to check on others, so I need you to keep it together. Help will be back again soon."

Caroline didn't wait to hear any response. She

rushed to the next victim. By the time other sirens approached a few minutes later, she had evaluated many victims.

Two were dead. At least two with severe injuries. A half dozen more with minor injuries that would require attention.

And a drunken jackass, still yelling, with a dislocated pinkie.

That first dead guy she'd come across had a couple of children's dolls in the back seat of his car. Somebody's dad was never coming home again. Yet a drunk driver who'd never even known he was driving the wrong way down a highway was going to be just fine.

Sometimes the world just wasn't fair. Caroline knew that much better than most by what had happened to her nearly two years ago.

This just reaffirmed it.

It was going to be a long, hard day.

TWELVE HOURS LATER, shift finished, having showered and changed at the hospital, Caroline made it home.

Except, it wasn't exactly home, was it?

It was the fourth place she'd lived in eighteen months, the place she'd moved into six weeks ago, but it wasn't *home*.

How could you call a place home when every time someone knocked on your front door it sent you into a panic?

Caroline stood in her driveway, looking up at her

town house's entrance, duffel bag swung over her shoulder, unable to go any farther. It had been the longest, professionally worst day she'd had in a long time. Her body was exhausted from the physical exertion of moving patients, administering CPR and going to one call after another today because of the fog. Her emotions were exhausted as the death toll had risen each hour.

By all means, she should go inside her house, fall into bed and be asleep before her head hit the pillow. Despite the deaths that couldn't be avoided, Caroline and the other paramedics had done good work. Had helped make sure the death count hadn't risen any further than it had. She should rest now. She deserved it.

But she couldn't seem to force her legs to move any closer to her empty house.

She knew she could call one of the officers over from the Corpus Christi Police Department to come walk through her town house for her. They would understand, and someone would come immediately.

Although not the person she really wanted—really *needed*—to be here. He wasn't part of the police force any longer. Zane Wales had hung up his white hat—literally and figuratively—the day they'd found Caroline raped and nearly beaten to death in her own home. The last victim of a serial rapist.

Caroline looked at her town house again, still unable to force herself to walk any closer.

What would Dr. Parker say? Caroline had been

uncomfortable talking to a psychiatrist here in Corpus Christi, so her friend Sherry had convinced her to speak—just once—to the Omega Sector psychiatrist over the phone. That "just once" had then turned into talking to Dr. Parker every couple of weeks.

If Caroline called Grace Parker right now—and she had no doubt Grace would take the call—would Grace tell Caroline there was nothing to fear? To just put one foot in front of the other?

No, she would tell Caroline that only Caroline could determine what would be the best thing to do. That pushing herself too far did more damage than it did good.

Her phone buzzed in her hand and she looked down to read the text.

How do you look in the mirror knowing your lies?

She rolled her eyes. Another one? This was getting out of hand. Caroline wasn't big on smartphones in general, so she didn't do a lot with hers. But she had to see if there was a way to block these texts.

The text was almost enough to distract her from her fear of entering the house. She took a step forward, then stopped, wiping her hand across her face.

She couldn't go in right now.

The thought frustrated her, but she let it go. It was okay. She would go to the Silver Eagle, a bar in town, and relax for a little while. A lot of the law enforcement and EMT gang hung out there. She could have a drink or a bite to eat or just chat. Get someone to show her how to block the annoying texts. When she was done, maybe she'd be more ready to face the big scary front door.

Once the decision was made, she didn't second-guess her choice, just jogged back to her truck, throwing her duffel in the passenger seat beside her. The ride to the bar didn't take long and she knew she'd made the right decision when she pulled into the lot.

Kimmie's little VW Beetle was parked here and almost every spot was full. Caroline would chat and unwind for an hour or two. She would face her town house when she was ready.

It had been a bad day. This would hopefully make it better.

She grabbed her purse, got out of the truck and made her way inside. The familiar smell of beer and fried food assailed her, as did the country music pouring at a perfect volume from the speakers. She smiled at Kimmie, who waved for Caroline to come join the people at her table.

Maybe being here wouldn't make her fears back at the town house just disappear, but nothing could make this day worse.

She glanced over at the bar as she walked toward Kimmie and almost stumbled as she found her gaze trapped by the brown eyes of Zane Wales. Compelling her, drawing her in, as always. She forced herself to look away from him.

Her day definitely just got worse.

Chapter Two

Zane Wales didn't come into the Silver Eagle very often. A lot of law enforcement guys hung out there, and generally Zane didn't need a reminder of what he no longer did for a living.

But today had been a long, weird day and Zane had found himself here an hour ago, rather than going straight back to his house on the outskirts of Corpus Christi. Just for a beer, a bite to eat. Hoping maybe none of the detective force would even be here.

They were *all* here.

If he could back out without any of them seeing him, he would've. But Captain Harris, along with Wade Ammons and Raymond Stone, both detectives Zane had worked with when he'd been on the force, waved him over to the bar where they sat as soon as they saw him.

Zane liked all three of the men—he really did. He chatted with them for a while before Wade and Raymond saw some ladies who interested them and said their goodbyes.

"How's the private aircraft charter business treating you?" Captain Harris asked as he took a sip of his beer.

Zane chewed a bite of the burger he'd ordered. "Today was different than most. A little crazy."

"How so?"

"Fog was causing problems up and down the interstate, so I got called for an emergency organ donation delivery. A heart. Flew it into Houston."

The entire flight had been tense—a very real deadline looming in front of them. Zane hadn't been sure if the deadline was because of the patient waiting for the heart or if the heart itself was only viable for so long. The two-person organ donation team flying with him hadn't said. They'd just told him the deadline.

Zane had gotten them there. Not much time to spare, but enough. He hoped the surgery had been successful.

"Yeah, fog was hell around here for us too this morning. Multicar pileup with a drunk driver. Half dozen other accidents that took up all our resources. Hell, even Wade and Raymond were out helping today."

That would've meant Caroline had a hard day. Not that he could do anything about that. Moreover, not that she would *want* him to do anything about that.

"Must have been a mess if you had to pull in Wade and Raymond."

"Sounds like your day was equally exciting. Heart

transplant. Important stuff. I'll bet you miss that on a daily basis when you're carting around cargo or rich people from place to place."

"Don't start, Tim." Zane already knew what was coming. A conversation they'd had more than once in the seventeen months and six days since Zane had quit the department.

"Son, I've known you since you were in elementary school. I had no hesitation at all about hiring you straight out of college or promoting you to detective, even after the trouble you got into in your younger years."

Evidently the man wouldn't be deterred. Zane raised his beer slightly in salute. "I know. And I appreciate it. High school was tough after Dad died."

"You can't tell me that running your air charter business means as much to you as chasing down criminals did."

Captain Harris was right; Zane couldn't say that with any sort of honesty. He enjoyed his business, loved to fly, loved working for himself, but it didn't challenge him the way working for the force had. Didn't challenge him nearly as much mentally or physically.

But Zane had lost his edge. Lost what had made him a good cop the day Caroline was attacked.

"I don't have it anymore, Tim. Don't have what it takes."

Captain Harris scoffed. "Don't have what, exactly?

You're still in just as good a shape. I know you have a permit for that concealed Glock you're carrying."

Zane didn't ask how the older man knew that. But he was right. Zane had never stopped carrying the gun, even after he'd quit the force. He just now had a different permit for it.

"I'll bet you have just as much practice on it and have aim just as precise as you did when you worked for me."

Zane shrugged one shoulder as he took a sip of his beer. "Just because I can hit what I'm aiming for doesn't mean I'm good as a law enforcement officer, Cap."

"Just because someone you care about got hurt doesn't mean you're not one," the captain shot back.

Caroline had been so much more than *hurt*.

"The rapist was right under my nose the whole time." Zane pushed his plate away, no longer interested in his last bites of food. "I shook the man's hand multiple times."

"Dr. Trumpold fooled us all," the captain reminded him. "Including that Omega Sector agent who came here to help us."

Zane just shrugged. "Jon Hatton did everything he could." But in this case, being part of an elite law enforcement agency like Omega hadn't been enough, either.

"And," the captain continued, "if I recall correctly, if you hadn't followed your instincts and gone after Hatton and Sherry Mitchell, Trumpold would've killed them both. That it was *your* bullet that put a stop to him."

Yes, Zane had stopped Trumpold. And hadn't lost a bit of sleep when he'd died in prison a year ago.

But that still didn't change one simple fact: Caroline Gill had opened the door to a rapist because she'd thought the knock on her door was Zane. Because Zane was supposed to be with her that night.

But he'd changed his mind at the last minute, wanting for once to have the upper hand in their tumultuous relationship. Stayed away as part of the head games the two of them played with each other all the time.

He would regret that decision for the rest of his life.

"If it had happened to someone else, you wouldn't blame them, Zane," Captain Harris continued. "Why are you holding yourself to a different standard?"

"It's not about standards. It's about my instincts. I can't trust mine anymore. And I won't put anybody else at risk."

"Zane, you need to—"

Harris stopped talking as the door to the bar opened and they both—engrained law enforcement instincts kicking in—looked toward it.

Caroline.

Zane hadn't seen her in a few months. They'd run into each other at a restaurant, a totally awkward exchange where they'd both been on dates, and their dates had both known Zane and Caroline used to be together. They'd said uncomfortable hellos and then spent the rest of the night trying not to notice each other.

Now Zane stared at her from where he sat, as always almost physically incapable of *not* looking at her. Taking in her long brown hair, pulled back in a braid like it so often was. The curve of her trim body filling out the jeans and fitted sweater she wore. His body responded, as it always had, wholly aware of her anytime she was around, in a completely carnal way.

What sort of pervert did that make him? Looking at Caroline—a rape survivor—with blatant sexuality all but coursing through him?

Just reinforced his decision to get out of law enforcement altogether. His instincts weren't to be trusted.

He knew the exact second she saw him, the slight hesitation in her step, but her gaze didn't falter. She didn't smile at him, but then again, he didn't expect her to.

Of course, he had to admit, even before the attack she hadn't always smiled at him. That was how their relationship had been: fire or ice. Never anything in between.

A friend called out to Caroline and she broke eye contact with him and headed in the caller's direction. Zane felt oddly bereft without the connection with Caroline.

He should've never come here in the first place.

He was about to ask for and pay the bill when Wade and Raymond came back over to sit with him and Captain Harris again. Raymond ordered them all another round before Zane could stop him.

"What happened to your lady friends?" Captain Harris asked.

"Married," Wade and Raymond both said at the same time, crestfallen.

"I might go talk to Kimmie." Raymond took a sip of the beer the bartender handed him.

Wade rolled his eyes. "Hasn't she shut you down enough times already?"

"Yeah, but she looks happier now. Especially since Caroline's here." Both men looked over at Zane as if they'd said something wrong.

"I wasn't going to hit on Caroline, man," Raymond was quick to announce.

He damn well better not.

Of course, Zane had no say over who Caroline dated. Although she better not go out with a horndog like Raymond Stone.

Zane shrugged. "Caroline can go out with whoever she wants." He forced his jaw not to lock up as he said it and carefully kept his fists unclenched. "Does she come in here a lot?"

Damn it. Zane wished he could cut off his own tongue. Why was he asking about her? But no one seemed to make anything of his interest.

"Not as much as we would like," Wade said. "I know Kimmie, her partner, invites her all the time."

"Kimmie's her partner? How long?"

"Awhile now," Captain Harris answered this time.

"I talked it over with the hospital staff and we thought Kimmie would be a good professional fit for Caroline."

"What sort of professional fit?" Maybe Kimmie had some sort of specialized training Caroline didn't have. But she looked awfully young for that to be the case.

Harris fidgeted just a little in his seat before looking away.

"What?" Zane asked. "Did Caroline need help? This Kimmie have training or something Caroline doesn't?"

Captain Harris shook his head. "No. Kimmie was pretty much brand-new. Anything she's learned outside schooling, Caroline has taught her."

That didn't surprise Zane. Caroline was stellar at her job as a paramedic. Could spot potential problems or injuries others would miss. Kept her head in a crisis. Had a way about her that kept people calm.

"So what was it about Kimmie that was a good fit for Caroline?"

Wade and Raymond glanced over at the captain, who was looking away. Then it hit Zane.

"Oh, Kimmie's a *woman*. That's why she was a good fit for Caroline. I guess nobody could blame her for asking for a female partner."

Now all three men refused to look at Zane.

Not all his detective skills had left him. "But she didn't ask for a female partner, did she? You just assigned her one."

Captain Harris pointed toward where Caroline and Kimmie sat, obviously easy and friendly with each other. "I've known Caro since she was born. Her parents are some of my best friends. So I did what I thought was right for her. She and Kimmie are a good team. It wasn't the wrong choice."

But it hadn't been *Caroline's* choice. And he would bet she hadn't liked it, no matter how chummy she and her new partner looked now. If Zane had been there, he would definitely have spoken up, at least told Captain Harris to talk to Caroline about it.

But he hadn't been there, had he? Zane grimaced. "I'm glad they get along," he muttered.

He saw Caroline glance over at them before quickly looking away and taking a casual sip of the beer the waitress had brought. She was just as aware of him as he was of her, although he doubted her awareness of him stemmed from attraction. Disgust at best, possibly even hatred.

So they both ignored each other, which everyone in the entire bar seemed completely aware of.

"I'm glad Caroline is finally going on a vacation," Wade said, trying to break some of the obvious tension. "She deserves it."

That was good news. "Where is she going?" Corpus Christi was a beach town and she'd always loved it. Did she still after what had happened? She used to live near the beach but had moved after the attack. Nobody in their right mind blamed her after someone had broken through her front door and viciously attacked her. Zane didn't know if she still even liked the beach at all.

Wade looked like he didn't want to answer. "How hard a question is it, Wade?" he asked the younger man, smiling. "A cruise? Tropical island? The mountains?"

Oh, hell, maybe she was going with another man. Maybe that was what Wade didn't want to answer.

"Who is she going with?" Zane could feel his jaw clench but couldn't seem to stop it.

He knew he had absolutely no right to be upset if she was going with another man somewhere. It was good—healthy—for Caroline to have other relationships. Someone important enough for her to move on with, to go on vacation with.

That was why he'd stayed out of her life for so long, right? So she would have a chance to move on, to put the past—including him and his part in her nightmare—behind her?

But damned if his hands didn't clench into fists as he waited for Wade's answer. As he prepared himself to hear the news that she really had moved on. That he had officially missed his chance.

"Just say it, Wade."

"She's not going with anybody, Zane. That's her whole deal. She said she wants time to be alone. Get away from the frantic pace for a week."

Zane refused to acknowledge the relief that poured through him at the knowledge Caroline hadn't found a man she was comfortable enough to vacation with.

He turned to Wade, rolling his eyes. "Why are you jerking my chain? I don't blame her for wanting peace and quiet. I guess that means she's not going to visit her family in Dallas. It's never peaceful around them."

Wade shrugged. "Nah, she's going hiking at Big Bend. She'll get plenty of quiet there."

Zane set the glass of beer that was halfway to his mouth back down on the bar. "She's going hiking in Big Bend Ranch State Park?" One of the largest parks in Texas, covering over three hundred square miles. Breathtaking views, multiple types of terrain. A hiker's dream.

Wade nodded. "Yeah."

"Alone?"

"Yeah, but she's been planning it for months. She's got a GPS that will let the park rangers know where she is at all times and has a course all planned out. She's super excited about it."

Wade continued to talk about how prepared Caroline was, how thrilled, but Zane tuned him out. He stood up. "Excuse me."

He turned and strode toward Caroline's table with definite purpose. There was no way in hell she was going on a weeklong camping trip by herself. Obviously none of her colleagues or friends were willing to tell her how stupid an idea this was.

Zane had no such problem.

Chapter Three

Her body was aware of Zane. She'd been conscious of him the entire time they'd been here, ignoring each other while totally mindful of each other's every move. They'd always been like that. Whether they'd been about to kill each other or fall into each other's arms, they'd always been *attuned* to one another.

She was attuned to him now. Aware of how damn virile and sexy he was. Not working for the Corpus Christi Police Department hadn't turned him soft or dimmed the edge of danger that had always surrounded him.

It drew her, just like it always had.

Damn him. Because the only thing that matched her passion for Zane Wales was her fury toward him. She'd like him to come over so she could slap him across his perfectly chiseled cheek.

And as if he could hear her and was going to call her bluff, he stood up and began walking toward her table.

"Holy cow, who is that?" Kimmie asked. "The guy that was talking to Captain Harris."

Caroline didn't say anything. But Kimmie's friend Bridget, sitting across from them in the booth, spun her head to the side so she could get a look at the eye candy.

"Ohhh." Bridget's eyes flew to Caroline. "That's Zane Wales. He's Caroline's."

Kimmie's face swung around to look at Caroline, shock evident in the wide circles of her eyes. "What?"

Caroline shook her head, her own eyes rolling at Bridget's remark. "He's not *mine*."

"Are you sure about that?" Kimmie looked back at Zane. "He sure is looking at you like he's coming for you."

"We used to date back in the day. It's been over for a long time." Zane had made sure of that.

Although she had to admit, it did look like he was coming directly to their table. But it most certainly would not be to talk to her. He'd gone out of his way to avoid her for the past eighteen months.

But five seconds later he stood right in front of their table, looking ridiculously sexy in his jeans and dark blue, long-sleeved collared shirt with sleeves he'd rolled up halfway to the elbow. November in Corpus Christi wasn't cold enough for a jacket.

He wasn't wearing his hat—that damned white cowboy hat he'd worn all the time. He was a Texan through and through and wearing it had been as natural to him as breathing.

He'd taken it off when he'd quit the force and she hadn't seen him in it since. Not that she'd seen him much at all.

He didn't need the hat. He wasn't hiding anything but thick, gorgeous hair underneath it. But Caroline missed him in it. Missed what its presence had stood for.

"Hey, Zane," Bridget purred. Caroline resisted the urge to slap her. Barely.

"Hey, ladies."

Caroline didn't know why Zane was at their table, but on the off chance it was to ask Bridget or Kimmie out, she couldn't stick around and watch.

"Excuse me." Caroline started to stand. "I've got to get going, you guys."

"Actually, I'm here to talk to you, if you don't mind," Zane said. He was looking directly at her now, closer than he'd been in nearly two years. She slid back into her seat, unable to draw her eyes away from his.

"Um, Bridget and I have to use the restroom anyway," Kimmie said, standing and grabbing the other woman's arm before she could protest.

Zane nodded at them as they left, then slid into the booth across from Caroline.

"Hi."

Of all the things she'd been expecting tonight, Zane coming over to chat with her hadn't been one of the possibilities. He'd withdrawn from her so completely over the past months that a conversation hadn't even been on her radar.

"What are you doing here?"

As far as greetings, it wasn't concise or friendly, but hell, nothing about Zane made her feel concise or friendly.

"I had some errands to run in town and thought I would grab a bite to eat."

He deliberately wasn't answering the question he knew she was asking. "Yeah, it looked like you were pretty close to done when I arrived."

He nodded and eased himself a little farther back in the booth, raising one arm up along the edge and knocking his knuckles gently along the column behind him. Damn the man and his comfortably sexy pose.

And damn sexy wrists exposed by his rolled-up sleeves. How could she have such a reaction from *wrists*, for heaven's sake?

"I wanted to talk to you," he finally said.

Her eyes flew to his face at that, in time for her to see his gaze slide over to his fingers that were still tapping against the column.

So whatever it was he wanted to say, he wasn't exactly comfortable with it.

"Spill it, Wales. Just say what you came to say." She honestly had no idea what it was. Her heart fluttered slightly in her chest that maybe he wanted to apologize for being so distant. For pulling away from her when she'd needed him. For keeping himself away.

Not that she'd forgive him and just let it go. Too much time and pain had occurred. But at least it would be a start.

His arm came down from the back of the booth and he leaned forward, placing his weight on both elbows. She couldn't break her gaze from his brown eyes even if she wanted to.

"Caro..."

Now she almost closed her eyes. How long had it been since she'd heard him call her by her pet name? The name he'd called her when they were alone. The name he'd called her when they were making love.

Unbidden, she felt herself leaning closer, desperate for his next words. It didn't have to be an apology; she knew the attack had cost him almost as much as it had cost her, although in a different way. Just some sort of acknowledgment that something had to change.

He cleared his throat, then continued. "You can't go on that hiking trip. Alone? That's absolutely stupid."

It took her a second to process his words. To realize what she'd hoped to hear from him wasn't anywhere near what was coming out of his mouth.

The pain reeled through her and stole her breath. Zane wasn't here to tell her they should be together; he was here to tell her she was stupid. She wrapped her arms around her middle, almost afraid she would fly apart if she didn't.

She looked away from him now, not even able to

look him in the eye. She was an idiot. Why would she think anything had changed?

"Did you hear me, Caroline? I really don't think this solo hiking trip is a good idea."

Did she hear him?

Did she hear him?

Fury crashed over her like a tidal wave, obviating the pain. It was all she could do to stay in her seat.

"Do I hear you, Zane?"

He had the good grace to look alarmed at her quiet, even tone. At least he still knew her well enough to know when she was about to blow a gasket.

"Caro…"

"Oh, no, you don't. Don't you dare call me that." The anger felt good, washed away the slicing pain of being wrong about him again. "You don't get to call me anything with any affection ever again."

Her words hurt him, she could tell, before he shut down all trace of emotion on his features. Good. She was glad she had hurt him. Glad she still could.

"Fine," he said. "I don't have to call you any friendly name to tell you that going hiking by yourself in the middle of the wilderness is just plain stupid."

Caroline looked over at the waitress who was walking by. "I need the check, please."

"I need mine too," Zane muttered.

The woman looked back and forth between them, a little concerned, before nodding. "Sure. I'll be right back."

"Where I choose to take my vacation is none of your concern, Zane."

"It is when no one is willing to tell you how risky and stupid it is."

Her eyes narrowed. "Really? How much do you know about my plans, exactly?"

"I know you're going hiking alone in Big Bend. That's enough."

Caroline clenched her fists by her legs and forced herself to breathe in through her mouth and out through her nose. She would not get in a screaming match with Zane Wales in the middle of a bar.

Unable to look at him without giving him the full force of her opinion—loudly—she surveyed the bar. Just about everyone was watching them, waiting for the fireworks. It wouldn't be the first time they'd provided a colorful show. But it had been a long time.

"You don't know anything about my plans, Wales. You don't know anything about my life. Remember?"

"You say that like me getting out of your life wasn't the best thing for you."

She just stared at him. "Seriously?"

"And regardless, this plan of yours—" he said the phrase with such derision her eyes narrowed and she felt her temper rising to a boiling point "—is ridiculous. You can't do it."

Oh. No. He. Didn't.

The waitress brought them both their checks and Caroline counted it one of her greatest accomplishments that she didn't say anything at all. She just got out a twenty-dollar bill, threw it down on the table and stood, not caring that she was tipping the waitress almost as much as the bill itself.

She felt every eye on her as she turned and walked out the door. She didn't care and definitely wasn't afraid to go back to her house now. She was too damn pissed.

She made it to her truck before she heard him.

"You can't seriously be going on this trip."

She didn't turn around. "You know what, Zane? You don't know anything about it."

"I know it's dangerous."

Now that they didn't have an audience, she didn't even try to keep her volume in check. "No, you're making a snap judgment that it's dangerous because you don't know all the facts."

"Then tell me all the facts."

Now she turned around. "I'm not stupid. And believe me, I have no desire to put myself at risk. I have taken precautions to make myself as safe as possible."

What was more, she needed this. Had talked extensively to Grace Parker about this time by herself. The psychiatrist had agreed that, with the right precautions for her personal safety, it was a good idea.

She would've told Zane all of this already if he'd been around. If he'd been a part of her life. But he hadn't been. So by damn, he did not get to have a say in her decisions.

"You know what? Just forget it." She spun back toward her truck.

"Hey, I'm not done talking to you."

"I don't give a damn if you're done with me or not. Have you thought of that? Maybe I'm done with *you* this time."

He strode directly to her. "What do you mean, this time?"

His nearness didn't bother her. Zane's nearness had never bothered her. This entire shouting match— so much like old times—was so freeing in a lot of ways.

"You bailed on me eighteen months ago, Zane. You don't get to have a say in anything I do anymore."

His volume rose with hers. "I didn't *bail* on you. I knew me being around you would be a constant reminder of the worst day of your entire life. So I tried to do the noble thing and get out of your way."

"Noble?" She all but spat the word, poking him in the chest. "You were too much of a coward to fight for us, so you ran."

"This discussion is not about the last year and a half. This discussion is about your asinine plan to go hiking for a week by yourself."

"Why do you think you get to have a say in what I do, Zane?"

She got right up in his face and shouted the words.

God, it felt so good to yell. To have someone yell back. To not have someone treat her with kid gloves like she was going to break any minute.

"You don't, Zane," she continued, poking him in the chest with her finger again as she said it.

His eyes flared as he wrapped his hand around her finger against his chest.

And then, before either of them realized what was happening, he yanked her to him and kissed her.

Caroline had been kissed since the rape. She'd even had sex with a couple guys since. But they hadn't been Zane. Hadn't been who, deep inside, she truly wanted.

And it sure as hell hadn't been a kiss like this.

Zane's lips were like coming home. His arms banded around her waist and hers slid up his chest and around his neck.

That hair. Thick and brown. She thought of how many times she'd flicked off his hat and ran her fingers all the way through it as he kissed her. Exactly like she was doing now.

He devoured her mouth and she couldn't get enough of it, pulling him closer with fists full of his hair, moaning as his fingers bit into her hips in his urgency to get her closer.

He backed her up until she was against her truck, then grabbed her by the hips and hoisted her up to the engine's hood. Now she could wrap both her arms and her legs around him.

Passion simmered through her blood as his lips nipped down her jaw to her neck. Not gentle, not timid. Just Zane. Fierce and passionate, the way lovemaking had always been for them. She moaned as one of his hands came up and fisted into her hair, holding her so he had better access to what he wanted.

Her.

And she couldn't get enough of it.

Dimly she was aware that they were still in the parking lot of the Silver Eagle. That any minute her colleagues, law enforcement officers who generally tended to frown on sex in public places, were going to make their way out.

This needed to be taken back to her place. Or his. Or a hotel room.

Stat.

"Zane, we've got to stop."

She sighed at another one of his nipping kisses, at the feel of him pulling her closer. She'd missed this so much.

But damn it, she didn't want to get arrested.

"Zane, stop."

She gripped some of his hair and gave it a tug.

She could tell the exact moment he came back to his senses. His hands dropped from her hair and he all but jumped back from her body.

But it wasn't until she saw his face that she understood. He was ashen. Distraught.

"Zane—" She reached for him, but he moved farther back.

"Oh, my God. Caroline, I'm so sorry. I don't know what came over me, I—"

She jumped down from the hood of her truck, desperate to wipe the distressed look off his face. Zane hadn't done anything wrong. He'd done everything right and she wanted more.

But at that moment Wade yelled from the open door of the bar. "Hey, Captain sent me out here to make sure the two of you hadn't killed each other."

Caroline rolled her eyes and turned toward Wade, waving her arm at him over the hood of her truck. "We're fine. Leave us alone and you guys mind your own business."

Wade's chuckle rang out in the still night air as he went back inside.

"So I wasn't saying, 'No, let's stop. I don't want to do this.' I was saying, 'Let's move this party someplace a little more...'" She turned back to Zane, her biggest smile in place.

But Zane was gone. She heard his truck start on the other side of the parking lot before his tires squealed as he sped onto the street.

Chapter Four

Zane woke from the nightmare, heart pounding, sweat covering his entire body despite the cool air coming through the screened windows of his bedroom.

He'd dreamed about the night Caroline had been attacked by Paul Trumpold a year and a half ago. It had been a while since he'd dreamed about it. Although it was no surprise that he'd had it again after what had happened in the parking lot of the Silver Eagle two nights ago.

He probably would've had the dream last night if he'd slept a wink.

The dream—really more of a memory—always started the same way: Zane sitting at his desk at the CCPD headquarters, even though it was late at night, doing some work, avoiding doing what he really wanted to do, which was accept Caroline's invitation to go over to her house when he got off work. He hadn't wanted to give her the upper hand in their relationship. Wanted to keep her a little off balance like she so often kept him. Wanted to let her know, for once, what it felt like to wonder what would happen next. She did it to him without even thinking. He wanted her to know—wanted *himself* to know—that he could do it to her.

It all seemed so ridiculous now.

The uniformed cop—a young kid, Zane couldn't even remember his name—who'd wanted to give Zane a heads-up before he got the official call had run up to Zane's desk, knowing Zane was lead detective in the case. The cop had been out of breath when he told Zane the serial rapist had struck again.

Zane always remembered that moment in his dream and in his life. Because that had been the last time he'd ever been okay. The last time his world had been whole.

He'd been pissed that the rapist had struck again before they could catch him, but his world had still had a foundation.

He could never stop the next moment in his dream any more than he could in real life: when the cop gave him the address of the rapist's latest victim.

Caroline's address.

He'd written down the first two numbers as the cop had said it out loud before he'd realized where it was, then had dropped everything and run as fast as he could to his car, driving way past the limitations of safety to get to Caroline's house.

Praying the entire time that there had been some mistake. That the address was wrong. That the kid cop, in all his excitement to be helpful, had gotten the numbers wrong or something.

The numbers hadn't been wrong.

The ambulance at Caroline's house had thrown him. He'd seen an ambulance there before, one Caroline had driven. Hell, she'd even driven an ambulance to his house to meet him for a quickie once.

But she hadn't driven this one. This time the ambulance had been *for* her.

The dream sometimes changed from there. He always had to cross her yard to get to the door of her house. Sometimes as he ran across the yard in his dream the ground swallowed him like quicksand, slowing him from reaching the door. Sometimes there were thousands of people all over the yard and he couldn't get through no matter how hard he tried.

Sometimes he ran as fast as he could, but the door kept getting farther and farther away.

But no matter what happened, the rapist—Dr. Trumpold—always just stood there laughing at Zane. And when Zane would finally fight his way to the door, the man would turn and whisper, "You know why she opened the door for me? Because she thought it was you knocking. Thanks for the help." Then he would disappear.

And in his place would be Caroline. Lying on the floor of her own foyer, beaten until she was unconscious. Clothes ripped off her small body. Being treated by her own EMT colleagues, handling her with care even though she was long past feeling any pain at that point.

Zane had just stared, watching his entire world lying broken at his feet. He hadn't been able to move, hadn't been able to say a thing, even if there had been something that could've been said or done.

In real life Zane had ridden in the ambulance with Caroline, had stayed by her side in the hospital until she'd finally woken up forty-eight hours later and helped them catch the rapist.

But in his dream he was always stuck there in the doorway of her house, looking down at Caroline's broken, battered body. Knowing she would never be okay again, that *they* would never be okay again.

And in the worst of the nightmares she would open her eyes from where she lay on the floor—although he knew that would've been impossible, since the blows from the rapist had caused both her eyes to be swollen completely shut—and echo her rapist's earlier comment, in an oddly conversational voice.

Where were you, Zane? I thought it was you knocking at the door.

And he would never have an answer.

He got out of bed now, knowing he wouldn't get any more sleep. Hell, he'd be lucky if he got any sleep any night this week after what had happened in the parking lot of the Silver Eagle.

He'd flown at least one flight each of the last fifteen days straight, so he should be glad he had nothing scheduled for today, but now he wished he could get back up in the air. After the nightmare, today wasn't a good day to be grounded. Zane wanted to be up in his Cessna.

Flying had been the only thing that had come even a little close to filling the hole in his life since he left the department. Like Captain Harris suggested, flying wasn't enough to completely eliminate the void, but it at least did something.

Zane wished he had another organ donor trip. That had been exciting. The deadline, the pressure, knowing someone was counting on you to get the job done.

That had been what his life had been like every day when he'd been a detective on the force.

Life when he'd had Caroline in it.

That wasn't any easier to think about than not being on the force any longer. Especially after what had happened in the Silver Eagle parking lot.

What in heaven's name had come over him? How could he have possibly treated Caroline like that?

They'd been fighting just like old times. Yelling at each other.

Then she'd poked him in the chest with that tiny finger of hers, just like she had so many times in the past. And in the past it had almost always ended with them on top of each other.

He had moved out of muscle memory more than anything else. Covered her finger with his hand like he had so many times before, moving in for a kiss.

Basic instinct, a primal need for Caroline, had taken over from there. He'd been so caught up in the kiss, knew she had been too. Had felt her hands in his hair, felt her legs pull him closer when he'd set her up on the hood of her truck. It had been so long; they'd been desperate for each other.

But then she'd told him to stop and his first instinct, the only one he'd been able to hear at all, had been to keep kissing her. Keep kissing that throat. That neck. Those lips.

Then when she should've slapped him, she'd simply tugged at his hair and told him to stop again.

And finally reason had returned.

He scrubbed a hand over his face now, despair tugging at him. He'd been holding her in place, unwilling to let her go.

Caroline, a rape victim.

He had to give her credit; she hadn't seemed panicked. She hadn't cried or punched him or run screaming back into the Silver Eagle. When he'd jumped back, she'd started to say something to him.

He could think of a number of things she'd had a right to say to him. And none of them were pretty. So when Wade had yelled whatever he had to say—Zane totally hadn't been listening—he'd gotten away from Caroline.

Because once again, as had been true for the past eighteen months, the greatest thing Zane could do for Caroline was to keep away from her. He'd made as quick an exit as he could manage.

She'd be in the middle of Big Bend State Park now,

on her hike. He still didn't like it. But she'd been right in one argument: what say did he have in her life?

None. Which was the best possible thing for her.

But the thought of her hiking alone still stuck in his craw. Maybe if he had kept his temper, used reason to discuss it with Caroline, he could've changed her mind.

But who was he kidding? *Reason* had never had anything to do with their relationship. Passion, fighting, yelling, heat. All those had. But never reason.

She'd driven him crazy from the moment they'd met in high school when her family relocated from Dallas. In both the best and worst of ways.

God, how he'd missed her the last year and a half. Missed the woman who had always stood toe-to-toe with him and refused to back down.

But now all he could picture was her broken body lying in the hospital bed eighteen months ago. Crying when she didn't know he could see her.

She'd never be able to go toe-to-toe with anyone again.

Not that Zane hadn't been willing to change everything about their relationship to fit her needs. Over those first few months, he'd tried. Went out of his way to be gentle, easy, light with Caroline. It had been weird, so different than what had always transpired between them. But for Caroline he'd been willing to do it. To do anything.

But it had all just seemed to make her upset. Sad, even.

Every time he'd let her win an argument, every time she'd poked him in the chest with that little finger and he'd just pulled her in for a hug, it had just made her more sad.

Finally, Zane realized that being around him at all made her sad. So he'd given her the only thing he'd had left to give: his absence. He'd quit the department, moved to the outskirts of town, made it so they never ran into each other.

And it had absolutely gutted him. His entire life became empty.

But for his Caro he'd been willing to pay that price.

And after his behavior two nights ago, obviously he needed to continue keeping himself away from her. The thought that he could've hurt her, scared her, brought back memories of her attack ripped a hole in him.

He started the day doing paperwork—owning your own charter flight company was perhaps the only business in the world that created more paperwork than law enforcement—but soon found he needed the release of some sort of physical activity. He decided yard work was in order. If his mother came by and saw the bushes and grass looking the way they did now, he would never hear the end of it.

And at least the hard, physical work of cutting and trimming allowed him to force the thoughts of kissing a stunning brunette—and how very good it had been before turning so bad—to the back of his mind.

He was going to have to see her in a couple of

weeks from now for Jon Hatton and Sherry Mitchell's wedding in Colorado, since Caroline was one of Sherry's best friends and in the wedding. But Zane would be damn sure to keep his distance.

He'd kept his distance for nearly two years. He'd keep on doing it now.

When his phone rang, Zane wiped the sweat from his head before removing his glove and grabbing the device. Speak of the devil; it was Jon Hatton.

Zane hit the receive button. "Hey, Jon, I was just thinking about you."

There was a short pause. "Well, I hope you weren't in the shower, because that would be weird."

Zane laughed. "No, just tackling some yard work that has been a particular pain in the ass."

Zane had met the Omega Sector agent here in Corpus Christi when the local police had needed help with the serial rapist case. He and Jon had solved the case, but too late for Caroline.

Jon had tried multiple times to get Zane back into law enforcement since Zane had quit, even talking to him about working for Omega Sector, but Zane hadn't budged. Although he had helped Jon with a couple of cases that had brought the man back to Texas.

"If you're calling to get me to help you pick out china patterns, I'm afraid I'm going to have to decline."

"As scary as that thought is, no, I'm not calling with anything about the wedding. We've got a problem, Zane."

Zane knew the other man well enough to know

that if Jon was calling him with "a problem" it was something serious.

"What's going on?"

"Can you get to your email right now?" Jon asked.

"Let me go inside." Zane grabbed the nearest dish towel from the kitchen and wiped as much sweat and dirt off his face and arms as he could before heading into his office.

"All right, I'm at my computer."

"I'm sending a picture of a Damien Freihof."

"I've never heard of him."

"He went to jail five years ago because he was about to blow up a bank full of people in Phoenix."

"Okay." Zane had no idea what this had to do with him.

"He escaped last year. Nearly killed Brandon Han and his fiancée, Andrea."

Zane knew Brandon; the man had helped figure out who the rapist was. But he didn't know about this Freihof guy or that he almost killed Brandon.

"That time—" it would've been right after Caroline's rape "—it's pretty fuzzy for me, Jon."

"Sure, man, I understand and don't expect you to know any of this."

"Okay."

"Freihof went to ground after he attacked Brandon and Andrea. He was injured in his own explosion. He resurfaced last week."

Zane still had no idea what this had to do with him. "Okay."

"I just sent you a picture of him."

Zane opened his email. "Okay, I got it." He studied the mug shot of Damien Freihof from five years ago. "I don't recognize him at all."

"I'm sending you another picture."

The second picture was a totally different man, roughly the same height and build but different jaw, eyes, hair.

"Okay, who's that?"

"That is also Damien Freihof."

"Damn." Zane whistled through his teeth. "He's good."

"Yeah, he is." Jon's tone held grudging respect. "Good enough to beat all our facial scanning software and to avoid the statewide warrant for his arrest."

"Do you think he's moved on to Texas?" If he had, it wasn't like Zane could do anything about it.

"Two days ago, Freihof masterminded a pretty elaborate plan. A bomb that killed one of our junior agents and put another agent in a coma. Looks like Freihof wants to make Omega Sector pay for putting him in prison. Plus, he nearly killed a mother and her toddler daughter in the process."

Zane's expletive wasn't pretty. "Sounds like this bastard doesn't care about collateral damage."

"Exactly. He wants as much collateral damage as possible. We've already been given that message. He's coming after people with ties to Omega. He's trying to hurt civilians we care about in order to split Omega's focus. I'm sending you one more picture."

The picture Zane received was of some sort of wall with a staggering amount of information on it: newspaper clippings, photos, drawings, police reports, Google search printouts, fingerprints.

"What the hell is that?" Zane couldn't make any sense of it at all.

"That's the wall of clues Freihof left for us. A very complicated puzzle that points out Freihof's next intended victims."

"How the hell were you able to make any sense of it?"

"It took us a long time, believe me." Jon paused for a second. "It looks like you and Caroline are on his intended victims' list, Zane."

"What?"

"There were very specific clues referring to you by name on the wall of clues. We think he might be coming after you soon, if he's not there already."

Zane's expletive this time was even uglier. "Caroline's off on her own."

"What?"

"She's on some damfool hiking trip in Big Bend State Park. Alone. Do you think this Freihof character might be aware of this?"

"Honestly, Jon, the man is a genius. I wouldn't put anything past him."

"Thanks for the heads-up, Jon. I've got to go. I'll keep you posted." Zane disconnected the call and was running for his bedroom, grabbing his go-bag. He would call Captain Harris on the way to the airport and get him to contact the park rangers at Big Bend and find out Caroline's exact GPS location.

He would file his flight plan and be in the air in less than an hour. He'd be with Caroline in under two. A madman genius had gotten to her once. There was no way in hell he was letting another.

So much for keeping his distance.

Chapter Five

Over the last few months, Caroline had been learning to trust her instincts again. Her instincts had told her a few months ago that this trip to Big Bend would be a healing one for her.

Now, nearing the end of day two, all alone with no one around for miles, she could honestly say she was damn happy she had followed her instincts.

She hadn't done it recklessly or without proper thought. She had planned. She'd considered. And finally, she'd just decided to take the chance.

Sort of like how she'd learned to do everything else in her life. She knew that bad things could still happen; people intent on harming others would always be around. Caroline did her best to prepare herself never to be a victim again, including multiple self-defense classes and hours of strengthening her body in the gym. She'd trained her mind to be more aware of what was going on around her so things didn't catch her off guard.

But ultimately after all the preparations, she had

to choose to just do it. To just do that thing that was a little bit risky.

To trust that she could handle it.

It wasn't easy. And ironically, if Zane hadn't come along at the Silver Eagle a couple of nights ago and told her she shouldn't do it, Caroline might have chickened out. But that had been the final push she needed.

"So suck it, Zane Wales!" she yelled at the top of her voice, since no one could hear her anyway.

She loved being out here in the open. Loved that there was a one hundred percent guarantee that no one would knock on her door—the one sound that threw her into a panic every time she heard it.

Why? Because there were no doors out here. Caroline grinned.

The door-knocking thing was something she and Dr. Parker had been working through. Grace warned her that it may always be a trigger, and if so, Caroline would have to learn to live with it.

She was proud of the progress she'd made. Proud of how far she'd come. Proud of her certainty that no man, no matter how big or strong, would ever be able to get the drop on her again. She may not win a fight, but she knew she wouldn't be the only person hurt at the end of it.

She just wished she could convince everyone else of that. Of her growth. She wished she could get people to treat her the way they had before the attack.

As much as she liked Kimmie as her partner, Caroline would've had no problem working with a man day after day. But Chief Harris—one of her parents' best friends and someone she'd known her whole life—hadn't asked her. He'd had clout with the Emergency Medical Service director and had just done what he thought was best.

Her parents and brother still couldn't talk about what happened to her. They had wanted to hire a full-time bodyguard for her. When she'd brought up fairly basic questions—with what money? Why would she need a bodyguard when her rapist had died in prison?—they hadn't had a good answer. So no bodyguard. But they still didn't treat her the way they had before the attack. Everything they said to her or did around her now was always tinted with some sort of combination of protectiveness, worry and pity, depending on the activity.

She hadn't told them about this trip at all. It just would've put them over the edge. She'd sworn Captain Harris—Uncle Tim—to secrecy too.

But she missed Zane most of all. She missed her friend, her lover, the person she spent hours arguing with about every topic under the sun. Of all the things she'd lost in the attack, the one she regretted the most was Zane.

Like everyone else, he hadn't known how to deal with what had been done to her. Hadn't known how to treat her. It had been even worse for Zane because he'd been the lead detective on the case and hadn't realized who the rapist was.

But hell, Caroline had worked with Dr. Trumpold for months and hadn't known it was him. They'd all been duped.

She'd needed gentleness for the first few months as her body had healed from the attack. But then she'd needed her life to get back to normal. Nobody seemed to understand that. Zane definitely hadn't understood it.

Their relationship had always been so tumultuous, almost emotionally violent. It was just how both of them were wired: live hard, fight hard, love hard. But when Caroline had been ready to get back to the fighting and the yelling and, yes, the lovemaking, Zane had already programmed himself to be something else. Something she didn't recognize. Didn't want.

And he'd quit the force. She'd been unable to fathom that. When she'd gone to his house, ready to fight him about it—honestly looking forward to the screaming match and whatever would come after it— he'd refused to engage. At all.

He'd offered iced tea and told her they should maybe talk later when they were both calm.

She could fully admit that she hadn't handled the situation well. That she'd told him she didn't want to be around him like that. That she didn't even recognize him. Didn't *want* to recognize him. To stay away from her until he could figure out who they were.

She didn't think he'd take it to mean she didn't want to ever be around him at all. But that had been the last time they'd been close to each other. Until a couple of days ago at the Silver Eagle.

She'd been such a fool thinking he'd seen the light, first when he came to talk to her and then when he'd kissed her. Zane Wales wasn't ever going to see the light when it came to her. So she wasn't going to pine for him any longer.

Instead, she was going to celebrate being out here by herself. Celebrate the development of another coping strategy. Celebrate being alive.

Trumpold had been escalating, and based on what Sherry and Jon had told her, he'd definitely planned to move on to killing.

Caroline knew, deep in her bones, she was lucky to be alive. That Trumpold hadn't been able to decide whether to kill her or not.

She was alive. She looked around at the stark landscape of the Big Bend. She loved it here. Loved the open, loved the vast skies, loved being alone in the late-afternoon sun.

She turned, annoyed at the sound of a plane flying relatively low overhead. A small plane, probably a flyby for tourists. Caroline just went back to gathering what she needed to build a small fire tonight for coffee and to warm up some of the food she'd hiked in with her. She also needed to check in with the park rangers. She did that every eight to twelve hours out of courtesy for her colleagues back in Corpus Christi. They'd get the report too and not worry.

She was tempted to tell them all to just bug off and

leave her alone, but she couldn't. These were people who loved her. She wished they wouldn't smother her with that love, but she couldn't fault them for it.

The plane came back by again and Caroline rolled her eyes. Big Bend was beautiful, but there wasn't enough to see for a double flyby. Then she realized the plane was landing not even half a mile from where she was camped.

Caroline grabbed her radio. She believed strongly in her independence, but she believed more strongly in not being stupid.

"Ranger station, this is Caroline Gill." She gave them her GPS coordinates. "I've just heard a plane land about a half mile south of me. Small aircraft."

"Yeah, we received a call from a Captain Timothy Harris in Corpus Christi."

"Captain Harris, yeah, I know him. Is there some sort of emergency?" She couldn't think of any reason Captain Harris would be on his way or have someone on their way if it wasn't an emergency.

"No, no emergency. He was clear about that. He was letting us know that a detective from his precinct was coming in via small aircraft. He said you wouldn't mind. Or that you probably would, but you'd get over it."

Damn it, Captain Harris was sending a babysitter. She wondered if her parents had gotten word of this trip. She wouldn't put it past them to browbeat Uncle Tim into sending someone to watch over her.

Well, whoever it was, she was sending them right back home.

She continued organizing her little camp, refusing to let anything get in the way of the peace she had found over the past two days. One of the things she'd worked very hard on with Dr. Parker was accepting what she had control over and what she didn't. Certain circumstances she had no regulation over. But how she responded to them was up to her.

She left her little camp and made her way the few hundred yards to the jagged edge of one of the cliffs Big Bend was known for with a stunning view of the Rio Grande river. She could feel her babysitter's eyes on her as he or she got off the plane and walked toward her, but she didn't pay any attention. Instead, she continued to stare out at the river as the sun began to dip in the sky.

Finally, she knew she couldn't avoid it any longer and turned back around.

And found Zane standing about twenty yards behind her. She froze.

"What are you doing here?" she stammered. Captain Harris had sent Zane to babysit her?

And what's more, Zane had actually agreed?

"I didn't mean to startle you. The ranger station was supposed to let you know I was coming." He took a few steps toward her.

"They did. I mean, they said Harris had called and told them someone was coming out here and to let me know. But I didn't know it would be you. What are you doing here?" she couldn't help but ask again.

"Right now? Enjoying the beautiful view."

Caroline turned back out toward the river. "Yeah, amazing, isn't it? The sun has set on the river this way for thousands and thousands of years. Makes you feel part of something much bigger than yourself."

Zane didn't say anything, simply absorbed. They stood in silence watching the sun drop farther, casting a purple hue throughout the entire area. Caroline just took it in with him. She had to admit, there was no one else in the world she'd rather share this moment with than Zane. She closed her eyes and felt the warmth of the setting sun on her face.

When she opened them again, she found him studying her.

"What?"

"Nothing. You look good. Peaceful, capable. Being here, at this place, obviously agrees with you. I was wrong to tell you not to come."

"You got that straight. I still don't know why you're here."

"I needed to make sure you were all right."

He stuffed his hands in his jeans pockets just like he always did when he wasn't telling the full truth. She'd never told him she knew that tell because she'd never wanted to give up the upper hand.

"You know I've been checking in with the rangers every few hours. You could've just asked them.

I'm sure some of the CCPD have, including Captain Harris."

He shrugged. "I needed to see it with my own eyes."

He still wasn't telling her everything, but she trusted him enough to know that if there was some true emergency he would've already hustled her off to the plane and gotten her out of here.

A thought struck her. "My parents didn't call you and make you come, did they?"

He chuckled. "No. I just wanted to see you for myself."

Her eyes narrowed. "You flew a long way just to look at me, Wales. You might want to consider taking a picture. It would be a lot cheaper."

"A picture of you, here, in this light couldn't possibly do this moment justice."

Damn it if the man didn't still know how to make her insides go gooey.

"Are you here to try to get me to leave?"

Zane looked around, taking in the vastness surrounding them. "No. I don't think there's any place else you ought to be than here right now. Like I said, it obviously agrees with you."

She shook her head and began walking back toward her little camp. She still didn't know exactly why Zane had come. He would tell her when he was ready. And honestly, as long as he wasn't here to try to make her leave her hike early, she didn't care. She didn't mind having him around. She'd never minded having him around.

"I can take care of myself, you know," she said without turning back to him.

"I'm beginning to see that more clearly," she heard him mutter.

Good. He should've seen it long before now.

Chapter Six

Zane didn't want to tell her his true purpose for coming.

He could admit he had been so wrong when he'd told her she shouldn't do this trip. He'd been arrogant and judgmental. She'd been right to get angry at him.

God, she looked so beautiful out here. At ease. Strong. Capable. With a Glock G22 in a holster at her hip.

Damn, if that wasn't just the sexiest thing ever. Like she'd been transported through time from the Wild West. A rancher's wife, ready to do whatever was needed to make her way securely through this wilderness.

"You know how to use that Glock you're carrying?"

She didn't even turn around. "Don't try to piss me off on purpose, Wales. You know I wouldn't be wearing it if I didn't know how to use it. I told you I wasn't coming out here unprepared."

Zane had no doubt what she said was the truth. If some sort of animal—four legged or otherwise—

threatened her, she would be prepared to protect herself.

Of course, she wasn't exactly prepared for a terrorist, one of Omega Sector's Ten Most Wanted, who might have set his sights on her. How did anyone prepare for that?

She looked so relaxed and peaceful he didn't want to tell her about Damien Freihof. Just because their names had come up on some psychopath's wall of clues didn't mean an attack was imminent. Zane would eventually have to tell her about the conversation with Jon Hatton, but not right now. Not when there obviously wasn't any danger out here.

Not when Caroline looked so peaceful.

He hadn't been lying when he'd said he just wanted to see her, to be with her. Hell, he'd wanted that for the last year and a half.

They talked about the weather, and how her hike had been so far. But at her small camp area she finally turned to him. "Okay, you obviously don't want to tell me the reason why you're here. And I'm assuming if someone was hurt at home, or if I was needed, we wouldn't be sitting around here chitchatting like a couple of old ladies."

Zane laughed out loud. Lord, how he'd missed her sharp tongue. "Nope, nothing like that."

"It's not Jon and Sherry, is it? Nothing's happened with the wedding?"

He stiffened at the mention of Jon's name, afraid

she'd ask for more specifics about him. "No, the wedding crazy is still in full gear as far as I know."

"Good. Because I'm rocking the bridesmaid dress Sherry picked out. She let us each choose our own style as long as it was the teal color she wanted. I got a halter style."

He had no idea what halter style meant but was glad to see her so excited about it. "Wedding is still a go, so your dress is safe."

She studied him for a long while.

"Well, it's getting dark, Zane. Have you seen whatever you need to see—that I'm alive and not throwing myself off the cliff, I presume—and you're leaving? Or are you going to stay?"

"Can I stay?" He did his best not to think too much about the question and what it meant for either of them. Right now he just wanted to be with her.

She shifted her weight onto one hip and stirred her fire with a stick. "It's a big park, Zane. I don't think I can stop you from camping here. Although I do think you're supposed to have a permit."

"You know what I mean."

"Do you have your go-bag?"

"Yep, plus a sleeping bag and MREs in the plane."

"Did you grab them for this trip or do you always have them in there?"

He knew she was still trying to ascertain exactly why he was here. "They're always in the plane. Although the go-bag is fresh."

"Meals Ready to Eat aren't very tasty."

Zane shrugged. "Some of them aren't too bad. And they're better than going hungry."

She smiled. "That's true. Maybe if you're lucky, I'll give you some of my food. Real stuff."

They hiked to his plane and got out his belongings. He showed her around the small prop plane.

"Do you like it? I never knew that flying was more than just a hobby for you before you started your business."

They had gone up a few times together over the years. Zane's grandfather had taught him how to fly in high school, and he'd gotten his pilot's license not long after he'd gotten his driver's license. Of course, Caroline's parents had categorically refused to let their only daughter up in a plane with a teenage pilot while she was in high school.

When she'd turned eighteen, she'd stopped asking their permission.

"I remember how your dad lit into me after that one time for taking you up." Zane got what he needed out and handed his sleeping bag to her. "You didn't tell me that you hadn't asked."

"I was eighteen, I didn't need their consent."

"Yeah, well, evidently your dad didn't know that."

That had been one of the last times Zane had flown with her, although not because of her father's threats to kill him. They'd both gone away to separate colleges, dating other people, but never seriously. When they'd both come back to Corpus Christi, things had gotten much more serious between them.

But that wasn't what he wanted to be thinking about right now.

"Anyway, my granddad left me the plane three years ago. And Jacob Scott was retiring from his air charter business, so I just took over. Worked out for everyone."

They started back toward the camp.

"Yeah, I'm glad that worked out," she murmured.

Her tone was sad, but he didn't push it. He didn't want to fight with her. Didn't want to do anything that would spoil this time and place with her.

DAWN THE NEXT morning broke just as gorgeous over the Rio Grande as sunset had left it the night before. And despite sleeping outside with no pillow, Zane woke feeling better than he had in a long time.

Eighteen months, nine days to be exact. The day Caroline had been attacked.

They'd spent the entire evening joking and fighting and arguing ridiculous points with one another about every topic from the Texas Rangers to the Rangers hockey team. Even when they were yelling the mood was easy between them. An underscore of happiness derived just from being with each other.

She didn't seem upset about how he'd treated her at the Silver Eagle. And, if it didn't upset her, then he knew he just needed to let it go.

He still hadn't told her about Jon Hatton's call. Honestly, there hadn't been any need to. Zane didn't want to ruin her trip for no reason.

But neither was he going to leave her here alone.

"So what's your plan, Wales?" Caroline asked as they shared breakfast consisting of oatmeal and dried fruit and some coffee she'd made over the fire. "You flew a long way just to camp out under the stars. I'm pretty sure we have those back in Corpus Christi."

Zane would've flown twice as far, hell, *more*, to have gotten the hours he'd had with Caroline. Hours where his presence didn't bother her. Where she was comfortable, confident.

"How would you feel about me paring down my gear and coming with you for a couple of days?"

Her eyes narrowed as if she was trying to figure him out. If she pushed now, he would have to tell her the truth about Damien Freihof. He'd have to tell her soon anyway.

"You got water in your plane?"

"Yeah. And a purifying bottle. It doesn't work quickly, but it will get out anything that will make you sick." It was standard equipment in his plane's emergency kit as well as some protein bars and the MREs.

Not to mention the Glock and extra ammunition he'd brought. The weapon was always nearby.

Of course, as he'd noticed yesterday, Caroline wasn't without her own weaponry.

"Okay, we might have to hunt a little small game to supplement our food if you decide to hang out more than a couple days, but I'm good if you are. Let's get camp packed up and ready to go."

And that was it. Just like old times, Caroline and her no-nonsense manner.

She broke camp as he went back to the Cessna and reloaded his go-bag. He took a moment to check in with Jon Hatton while he was away from her.

"Everything okay with Caroline?" Jon asked by way of greeting.

"Yes, no problems. It looks like your Freihof guy either doesn't know she's out here or has decided not to make a play. But I'll still be keeping my eyes peeled."

"Last time he used someone else to do a lot of his dirty work, Zane. So just be careful."

He finished his conversation with Jon, then hustled back to Caroline, who was ready to go.

She turned to him, everything already packed up. "What were you doing back there, writing poetry? Let's get a move on, Wales."

Her tone was annoyed, but he saw her smile as she turned away.

"No, I was fixing my hair if you must know. Beauty like this doesn't come without a price." He heard her guffaw as they began their hike. The only trace of the camp was the small ring of ashes from their fire. In wilderness camping you carried all your supplies in and all your trash out.

Big Bend advertised itself as "the other side of nowhere." Over three hundred square miles of all sorts of terrain: rolling hills, cliffs and valleys, desert sections as well as green hills. A hiker's dream if you wanted a variety of terrain and a chance to be alone. Especially now in November. No families camping or large groups led in on horseback.

Caroline had obviously planned out where she would be going. She had a map she glanced at every so often, a compass she brought out more to make sure they were on track. She was prepared, gutsy and strong. Just like she'd always been except...

The image of her rape, of seeing her lying unconscious on the floor, swamped him. Stole his ability to breathe, to do anything but flounder in remembered panic. In the knowledge of how scared and hurt she had to have been.

She chose that moment to look over at him.

"You okay there, cowboy?"

He tried to shake it off, to make a joke. But he couldn't. He couldn't say anything. He just stopped and stared at her.

Somehow she understood.

"Zane, we're here. We're both here and we're both good."

He just nodded.

"I need you to be in the *now* with me, okay?" she continued. "The *then* costs too much. Takes too much. Be with me—with who I am—*now*."

She reached up and touched his cheek. He stared at her for a long moment before turning his lips to the side and kissing her palm. They both nodded.

She didn't want to stay in the past. He sure as hell

couldn't blame her for that. She didn't want him to keep her there, either.

He realized he'd been doing that for a year and a half. Keeping her inside the box of the attack.

She turned and began walking again.

Obviously she refused to stay in the box any longer. He needed to stop trying to fit her there.

They walked the next few hours chatting easily, at least mentally. Physically, the pace they set as they hit higher ground made talking more breathy.

Midafternoon, Caroline stopped abruptly.

"Everything all right?" he asked.

"Yeah." She nodded. "Just get out your water and let's take a drink."

They'd just stopped for water less than twenty minutes ago. Zane didn't mind stopping, but this seemed odd. Caroline took a swig from her canteen, then walked around so she was standing on the opposite side of Zane.

"Caro, what's going on?"

"I think you better tell me why you're really here."

"Why do you ask that?"

"Because for the last hour there's been someone following us. And I just caught the reflection of the sun off a riflescope again. Whoever it is is getting closer."

"Damn it. You're sure it's not just some other hikers also out here?"

She shook her head. "That's what I thought at first. I'm not sure that the person means us any harm, but someone is definitely following us. Hikers aren't out here for company. Plus, we're on a route I created, not one on any of the normal trail maps. The chances of anyone picking the exact same route I did is pretty slim."

Zane grimaced. Caroline was right. This didn't sound good.

"If you weren't here, I'd double back, sneak behind them and see what was going on."

"Do you think it's just someone in trouble?" Even as Zane said the words, he knew it wasn't true.

"If they fired that rifle in the air, I'd be back to them in no time offering assistance. Whoever it is isn't in trouble. They're gaining in speed."

Zane saw a patch of light shine onto Caroline's shoulder before it quickly moved away. She didn't look at it, although she had to have seen it.

"Was that their scope again?"

She took a sip of water again, looking at him casually, not giving any hint as to the seriousness of the conversation. "Yep. Not someone very familiar with it if I had my guess. I would imagine they're looking at my face right now. Trying to figure out why we stopped."

"Are you in range for them to shoot?" Zane casually stepped to the side so the rifle would be trained at his back, not at Caroline.

"No. If they don't even know they're giving off a glare, I don't think they would try a long-range shot.

Right now they're just keeping us in their sights for whatever reason."

"Good."

"So you want to tell me why you're really here so we can formulate a plan and figure out what we need to do?"

Zane hadn't wanted to tell her. Hell, twenty-four hours ago he would've worried that maybe she wasn't strong enough to handle it. He'd been damn wrong about that.

"Jon called me yesterday. He was worried about us."

"Us? Why?"

"Looks like some guy pretty high on the public enemy list has decided to make you and me targets."

Chapter Seven

Caroline appreciated the matter-of-fact way Zane gave her the news. Didn't pull any punches, didn't sugarcoat due to any misconceptions of what might be too much for her *delicate* feelings. He treated her the way he did before the attack.

The news was a little scary, she could admit. Some guy who had already killed or injured multiple Omega Sector agents now seemed to be targeting people who had an attachment in some way to Omega.

And she and Zane specifically. Not awesome.

"So does Jon think this Freihof guy is here now at Big Bend? Is that our rifle friend back there?"

"It seems as though Freihof's MO is to get other people to do his dirty work for him. So it may not be Freihof himself."

Not being here himself wouldn't make them any less dead if the rifle guy started shooting at them. "So what's our plan?"

"First we radio in to the park rangers. See if they

know anything about anyone else out here. Maybe it's just someone like you who'd planned to be here the whole time."

She shrugged. "Okay. And the truth is, if the person wanted to shoot us outright, he could've done it before now. We weren't moving fast enough to escape someone."

Zane nodded and looked casually over his shoulder in the direction where she'd seen the rifle glint. "Let's try to put a little distance between us and whoever that is, okay?"

As they restarted walking, Caroline set a pace that was fast but not fast enough to look like they were deliberately trying to get away. Zane contacted the park rangers and they found out no one had filed a hiking plan in this direction but Caroline.

It didn't mean definite bad news, but it wasn't good news, either.

"Damn it, I'm going to have to cut my trip short, aren't I?" She'd been looking forward to this for so long.

"How about when we get this Damien Freihof thing settled, you and I will come back out here for a long weekend?"

Caroline almost stopped midstep at his words. Definitely not what she'd been expecting him to say. She still wasn't sure if he was inviting himself along because he wanted to look out for her or because he wanted to be with her.

But at least he was willing to be in her presence

and not treat her like she was about to break. That was all she'd ever wanted from Zane.

She glanced over at his six-two frame, dark brown hair and muscular build. Okay, maybe it wasn't *all* she'd ever wanted. But it was a start.

"I don't know, Wales. What about all the hair product you'd need for a whole weekend? Think you have a backpack that sturdy?" She looked over her shoulder at him.

He grinned and winked at her. "Maybe I'll wear my hat."

Caroline's stomach did the craziest little somersault as much from his smile as his words. She would give anything to see that old cream-colored Stetson back on his head. Even if it didn't mean he was going back to work for the police department. It would just mean he hadn't given up on himself. On life. On there being good in the world.

Whatever it had meant when he'd stopped wearing it.

She smiled back. "Then it's a hiking date."

Less than an hour later, both of them knew they were being hunted. "Whoever it is is gaining," Zane said to her.

"Yeah, I noticed. But I've got a plan formulating. How do you feel about rappelling?"

He gave her a sidelong glance. "I've done it a couple of times, why?"

"There's a cliff edge coming up that has some rappelling ropes and gear already in place. I wasn't planning on using it this trip because it's dangerous alone, but it would get us back down to the river, where we can circle back around to your plane."

Zane glanced back over his shoulder again. "You think we should just give up all appearances of not knowing someone's following us and just make a run for it?"

"Yep. It's our best bet against someone who has a rifle compared to our sidearms. No way we're going to get the same range. We don't want to take a chance on getting into a firefight."

"Smart."

She shrugged. "You know we might be making a mountain out of a molehill. The difference between binoculars and a riflescope is impossible to tell from a sun reflection."

Zane glanced over his shoulder. "You could be right. But to be honest, I'm not willing to take that chance. Not when the person has been steadily gaining on us despite this pace."

"Yeah, my gut says we need to bail. Fast. And if there's one thing I've learned, it's to listen to my gut." It had been one of the first things she and Dr. Parker had worked on: learning to trust her instincts again.

"I agree."

"I say we ditch the packs and run. We can ask the park rangers to come out for them later. Given the psychotic killer possibly targeting us and all, they probably won't mind a trip out here to observe."

He was already stealthily unbuckling his backpack. "They'll probably only laugh at us a little bit."

"Let's hope it's nothing and we can all chuckle. The cliff is about a quarter mile from here. Are you ready to go on my signal?"

He nodded. "Yep, call it and we ditch the packs and run."

They were still walking, but now both of them had moved their hands to the buckles of their backpacks, after Zane grabbed a couple things as casually as he could from the outer side pocket of his. Caroline could feel eyes on them. She unhooked the small strap across her shoulder and moved her hands to the larger one at her waist.

"Now!" she said through gritted teeth. She pulled at the latch at her waist and the pack fell heavily to the ground. Zane's did the same. They both sprinted toward the cliff wall.

Not five seconds later a bullet bit into the ground behind them. Not close enough to be life-threatening, but definitely enough to prove the other visitor definitely wasn't just some lost hiker.

Zane cursed as two more shots hit the ground behind them, ricocheting off the ground. Caroline didn't know if the shooter was just a bad shot or what; she was just glad he wasn't cutting off their route to the cliff edge. As a matter of fact, the shooter was almost guiding them that way.

Because the guy hadn't studied Big Bend like Caroline had. Didn't know there was rappelling equipment at this particular cliff. He thought he was trapping them, but he wasn't.

She and Zane dived behind a large boulder at the edge of the ravine, giving them some cover. No more shots rang out.

He tucked his head to the side and grimaced. "Park rangers are definitely not going to laugh at us."

"Let's just hope we make it back to them."

The rappelling harnesses lay inside a box next to the boulder. They didn't waste any time getting them onto their bodies and clipping the carabiners onto the rope. Zane snatched his shirt off and ripped it into four pieces.

"We need gloves, but this will have to do. We'll burn our hands otherwise."

Caroline took the material, grateful he'd thought of it. She wouldn't have until she'd been over the cliff.

"Do you think he's heading toward us?" she asked as she wrapped the material of the shirt around her hands and refused to gape at how ridiculously sexy Zane looked in just his jeans with no shirt on.

"I think he thinks he has us trapped, so he's probably not hurrying. And might even think we'll be laying down some cover fire. But I don't think we should waste any time."

"He probably doesn't know about the rappelling."

"Let's hope not."

They kept as low as possible as they had to leave the cover of the boulder in order to clip into the rappelling rope. Caroline expected a few more shots but heard nothing.

"It's been a while since I've done this," she admitted as she clipped in and looked over the side of the ledge. Forty yards was a long way to fall.

"Yeah, me too. But it's better than being shot at."

As if the shooter could hear their conversation, a shot rang out near the boulder where they'd just been.

"Take it slow and steady," he told her. "Ready?"

They both got to the edge, then pushed backward, leaping straight back from the top, letting rope go slack as they both slid down about eight or nine feet, then stopped themselves with their hands as they caught their weight against the cliff wall with their feet.

"Good," he told her. "First leap is the hardest. Let's keep moving."

He didn't have to tell her twice. Caroline was well aware of how precarious their situation was if the rifle guy figured out they were no longer behind that boulder and were making a getaway. They would be sitting ducks if he came to shoot at them while they were rappelling down the side of the cliff.

They moved as quickly as their lack of real gear would allow. Caroline was thankful again for the pieces of shirt wrapped around her hands.

Halfway down she began to really believe they were going to make it. She wished she could be doing this under different circumstances because it would be a lot of fun.

She looked over to see Zane grinning like an idiot and knew he felt the same way as she did.

He reached over to high-five her.

Which saved her life as her rope came unattached to its place at the top of the cliff. She immediately began to tumble backward, falling with nothing to catch her and yards to go before the bottom of the ravine.

Zane grabbed for her with his free hand, his quick reflexes allowing him to catch her wrist. Caroline immediately wrapped her fingers around his wrist in a vise and swung her other hand up to latch on to him too.

There was no smile on his face now as he used all his strength to hold on to her.

"I'm okay," she said, and he nodded. She could see sweat breaking out all over his forehead at the exertion of holding both of them.

Suddenly Zane's line jerked also.

Zane said nothing, just pulled her up so they were torso to torso and she could wrap her arms around his shoulders and legs around his waist. He began sliding them both rapidly toward the ground. There was no way he could leap out to get slack on the rope without slamming her against the cliff, so he had to use sheer muscle to get them down.

A few seconds later his rope jerked again, dropping them both five feet.

"Your rope can't hold us both."

"It'll hold," he said through gritted teeth, continuing to work them down. Caroline just tried to keep herself still to not make his job any harder.

The rope sustained them until they were less than ten feet off the ground. Then it gave way with a gentle hiss just as hers had. With nothing now to hold them at all, they both fell backward, landing hard on the ground.

Caroline lay for long seconds just trying to get air back into her lungs, unable to move.

Finally, she looked over at Zane. He was alive, conscious.

"Okay?" he wheezed.

She nodded.

He stood and helped her to her feet, both of them still struggling to take in air. As he wrapped his arm around her shoulders, he began moving them to the east.

"We've got to get back to my plane, but we're going to have to circle around backward to do it. The rifle guy has the higher ground. It won't take him long to figure out we're down here, and once he does, he's definitely going to try to pick us off."

They kept as close to the cliff wall as they could, trying not to give the shooter a target. Without the packs they could move much more lightly and quickly. The hike that had taken them four hours took just half that going back with the punishing pace they set for themselves.

They both had their water canteens, and Zane had grabbed a protein bar before ditching his pack, which they shared without stopping. They never let up the pace even when no shots were fired. Caroline still couldn't shake the feeling that they were being watched.

But that didn't make sense. If this Damien Freihof—or whoever he was working with—was still after them, he would've been shooting. Even if he wasn't good enough to kill them at that distance, he could've still kept them pinned down.

But even though Caroline didn't see any more reflections off riflescopes, she couldn't shake the feeling that danger was only a step behind them.

Zane must have felt it too, because he never once suggested they slow down or that they might have shaken the shooter.

The sun was beginning to set as they got to the plane. They approached it together, both of them with their weapons drawn.

No one was there. No evidence the door had been tampered with or of any problems. Zane did a more thorough check, making sure there weren't any leaks or noticeable trouble before jogging back to her.

"Let's get out of here," he said to her, opening the hatch door so she could climb through. He followed immediately behind her, grabbing a shirt from a small backpack he had in the cockpit. "I know it sounds crazy, but I feel like we're about to be ambushed at any moment."

Caroline shook her head, still looking through the

window. "No, it's not crazy. Even though no one has been shooting at us, I feel the same way."

They buckled themselves into the harness-type seat belts and slipped on the communication headphones as Zane started the engines. He eased the plane to the farthest end of the open area where he'd landed. Caroline held on to the seat belt straps where they crossed over her chest as he eased the throttle back and sent the plane speeding down the field. Moments later they were airborne.

As they climbed into the air, she relaxed. She had no doubts whatsoever about Zane's ability as a pilot.

"Okay, I have to admit I was expecting bullets to be flying at us or something," Zane said into the headphones.

"Yeah, me too."

"I've got to call in to the nearest air traffic control. Declare an emergency flight plan. There's going to be a crap ton of paperwork to fill out with this, but—"

A deafening roar and loud popping sound came from the engine to their left before it stuttered to silence.

"What just happened?"

"Engine flameout," Zane said, both hands wrapped in a death grip on the steering column, struggling to keep the plane steady. "We can still fly with one engine, but it's not optimal. I'll need to inform ATC so we can declare it and get back on the ground as soon as possib—"

His words were drowned out by another roar, this

time from the right engine. Caroline could see the glare of the flames out of the corner of her eye for a minute before it went out.

Now they were flying with no power in either engine, the silence in the cockpit giving new meaning to *deafening*.

Zane struggled to control the Cessna at all now. "Get the radio and call out a Mayday." He nodded toward the GPS unit between them. "Give them our closest coordinates."

Caroline grabbed the radio and turned it to the frequency she'd used for the ranger station. No one was manning it, since it wasn't her check-in time, but she kept repeating the Mayday and coordinates just in case.

She could see Zane looking around for anywhere they could possibly land. Big Bend wasn't set up for planes and most of the ground wasn't flat, especially in the direction they'd been heading before the engines blew.

"What do we do?" Caroline asked. It was much easier to hear her now with no engine noise.

"We need to find a place to put her down. Fast. Any open area. No big rocks or trees."

That wasn't going to be easy.

"I think that dried-up riverbank is our best option. It's probably our only option." Zane motioned to the left with his head and maneuvered the plane, almost by sheer willpower, toward it.

"C'mon, baby," he muttered as the plane shuddered

slightly, resisting his ease toward the opening in the earth in front of them.

An eerie shadow joined the already eerie enough quiet as the plane dipped lower and cliff walls surrounded them on either side.

"Caro, we're going to be coming down fast and hard. Make sure your harness is on as tightly as possible." Zane did the same to his own.

Caroline did all she could do, which basically was not scream at the top of her lungs and distract Zane, as the ground kept moving rapidly toward them. He needed every bit of concentration he could get.

"You can do this, Zane."

She didn't know if he heard her as the Cessna hit roughly along a higher section of the creek bed, then bounced hard against the ground. The force flung Caroline back against the seat as the plane flew back up, then came down roughly again. The impact was bone-jarring, but at least they were still alive.

Zane slowed the plane as much as he could and then turned the yoke sharply so they began to slide to the side. Working against their own speed snapped them around hard, collapsing one side of the plane as the landing gear gave out, slowing them down. She didn't know if it would be enough to stop them from slamming into the ravine wall.

Zane took his hands off the yoke; there wasn't anything he could do to steer now. The weight of the plane teetered forward as they continued their rapid approach toward the wall.

He reached out his hand to grab hers. "Hang on, we're going to flip," he said. Caroline grasped his hand, doubtful they'd live through the next thirty seconds.

The plane flipped, ripping their hands apart as they slammed into the ravine wall.

Then there was only blackness.

Chapter Eight

Zane's eyes opened and it took him a minute to get his bearings. He was hanging in the seat sideways, the harness holding him in. The entire cockpit tilted at a precarious angle. But he was alive.

His attention immediately focused on Caroline. Her much smaller body may not have withstood the impact so well. He couldn't see her from where he was trapped against the seat. Now that the plane had flipped, Caroline was above and a little bit behind him. And the plane was rapidly filling with smoke.

"Caro?" Nothing. "Caroline? Talk to me."

He pushed himself up from the seat so he could get a glimpse of her. She hung limp against the harness holding her, her arms and her hair just fell forward, lifeless.

Zane forced panic out of his system as he reached down to unhook his safety harness. After a tug-of-war of brute force, Zane won. He slipped his arms from the belts, ignoring the pain, grateful he could move at all.

"Wake up, Caroline. Can you hear me?" She still hadn't moved or said anything.

He worked his way up to Caroline's seat, where she lay motionless against the belts. He didn't see any blood or any obvious injuries but knew they could be internal.

He was reaching for her pulse when she moaned and moved slightly. Zane felt relief wash through him. She wasn't dead.

But smoke was definitely filling the cockpit at an alarming rate. He needed to get them out of the plane immediately.

"Caro? Baby, can you hear me? We're alive, but we've got to get out of here."

He tried pulling at the release mechanism of her harness, but it was jammed. Breathing was getting more difficult.

Zane grabbed his army knife from his jeans pocket. Bracing his legs against the small side window, which was now on the ground, he used his strength to lift Caroline's unconscious form, then sawed through the canvas of the harness belts.

It wasn't an easy process. Even as light as she was, holding her dead weight up so he could cut the straps without cutting her took all his strength. The smoke was really becoming an issue. It was coming from the back of the plane, but once it hit the engines, this thing would be a fireball.

He felt one of Caroline's arms brace herself on his shoulder, holding part of her weight. He looked up from where he was cutting the straps to see her green eyes peering down at him.

"Hey."

"We're alive," she whispered.

"Yes. But it's just a matter of time before the fire makes its way to the engines. We've got to get out of here."

"You're bleeding." Her voice was tight.

He looked over at his arm where he'd been cut. "I'll be fine. Push yourself up as far as you can."

"I can only do it with one arm, I'm pretty sure the impact knocked my other shoulder out of joint."

Zane muttered a curse. "Okay, just hang in there."

She grimaced at his poor choice of words.

Cutting the side where she could hoist herself became much easier with her assistance. He had to brace his arm against her chest and push to get the other side. He could tell by her labored breathing that his actions were hurting her. When the last of the belts finally gave way, she fell heavily on him. He caught her as gently as he could.

"You okay?" She nodded and he put her gingerly on her feet and helped her gain her balance as he began to climb over the pilot seats. Both of them were coughing now.

"Let's get out of here," Zane wheezed. He grabbed his small backpack—it didn't have much in it in the way of usefulness, but it was better than nothing.

He pulled himself up and through the flimsy cockpit door that had broken away and into the main cabin, reaching back to help Caroline. They could both see flames now.

"I'm fine," she told him. "You get the outer door open. I'll get myself out of here."

Zane nodded and proceeded to put all his effort into opening the door that would lead them outside. It was caught against the ravine wall and didn't want to budge. When using his back and shoulders didn't do much, Zane leaned his weight against one of the passenger seats and used the muscles in his legs to try to force open the door. Caroline made her way out of the cockpit and added her strength to the effort.

Damn it, they couldn't survive the crash just to die here from smoke inhalation.

Their eyes stung and lungs burned, but finally the crushed door gave way on the hinge side and slid open enough for them to fit through. Zane steadied her as much as he could as they half ran, half stumbled away from the burning plane.

He knew the moment his livelihood blew up. The force literally swept them off their feet and threw them forward onto the ground. He heard Caroline cry out as her injured shoulder hit the ground hard. Zane wrapped his arm up over her head as pieces of the plane became projectiles all over the ravine.

The quiet after the explosion was unnerving. Both of them lay on the ground trying to catch their breath for a long while. Finally, Zane flipped himself over and sat up, gently helping Caroline to do the same.

She reached over and touched her injured shoulder, wincing. "Definitely out of the socket. It's going to need to be put back in."

That didn't sound good in any way. "Like you running into a wall and knocking it into place?"

She rolled her eyes. "You've seen *Lethal Weapon* too many times. No, the acromioclavicular joint can be eased back into place with much less violence."

He noticed she didn't say with much less pain.

"You're going to have to do it, Zane."

"Hang on a second, I'm not the medical professional. You are." Plus, the thought of hurting her made him almost physically ill.

"I can't do it. It takes two hands to slip the joint back in properly."

She was already looking pale, and he could tell every time she gave a residual cough from the smoke it was causing her more pain.

"I don't want to hurt you."

She took a step toward him. "Once you do it, it will hurt a lot less, believe me. And there's no way I'm going to be able to climb out of here with a dislocated shoulder. Plus, the longer we wait, the more swollen and aggravated it will get. It's an anterior dislocation, so that's good."

He didn't know what that meant, but didn't see anything good about it.

"I'm going to lie on the ground so there's no weight on this shoulder." He helped her get down on the ground as she explained what he needed to do. Which way to pull her arm and which way to twist once he did. He knelt down next to her injured arm.

She reached up with her good arm and pulled his face down so their foreheads were touching. "Thank you," she whispered. "Remember, slow and easy, no quick, jerky movements."

He shifted slightly and kissed her forehead. It was time to get this done so both of them could stop hurting. "Ready? One, two, three."

Zane did exactly as she'd instructed, wishing to God roles were reversed so he could take the pain instead of her. He heard a broken sob come out of her mouth at the very last moment before the joint slipped back into place.

He wiped her hair off her brow as her breath shuddered out. But he could tell immediately by the way all the muscles in her body relaxed that she was in much less pain now.

"Thank goodness," she murmured.

"Does it still hurt?"

"Not nearly as much as it did thirty seconds ago."

They both sat there, just catching their breath.

"How about you? Are you okay? I know you have that cut on your arm."

He looked down at it. "It's already stopped bleeding."

Zane did a physical inventory of the rest of his body. Everything seemed to be moving, even now that adrenaline wasn't fueling all his thoughts and actions. No sharp or overwhelming pains, but a ton of little ones.

"You doing okay?" he asked her.

She grimaced and didn't open her eyes. "My entire body hurts, but I don't think I have any life-threatening wounds."

"That's basically how I feel."

Now she opened her eyes. "But considering we just crashed into a ravine, I think we're in pretty good shape."

"Damn straight."

They both sat up although neither of them were very interested in doing more. "How exactly did that happen anyway? I'm going to assume that us being shot at and then both engines of your plane blowing out on the same day are not a coincidence."

Zane shook his head. "There's no way in hell it's a coincidence. If one engine had blown, I might have called it suspiciously bad luck. Both engines? That's sabotage."

They both stared off at the wreckage in silence for long minutes. "I know you didn't have time to do a full walk-through before we took off, but did you see anything suspicious?"

"No." Zane stretched his shoulders, trying to work out some of the stiffness. "I looked for obvious problems—leaking fluid that would signify cut lines—but didn't see anything. But if someone knew about planes, there are easy ways—like putting sugar in the gas tank, which clogs the fuel lines as it dissolves—to bring a plane down."

"Now we know why our shooter didn't take any more shots at us. He wanted us to make it back to the plane."

Zane nodded. "And now we know we're likely dealing with more than one person. Someone with the rifle and someone who sabotaged the plane. And I don't think it was coincidence that our rifle friend decided to wait until we were at the rappelling equipment before taking his first shots."

Caroline grimaced. "He was leading us there."

"Yep. And then that equipment just happened to be faulty? I don't think so." Zane shrugged and stood. "We've had two attempts on our lives today and neither of them have been by rifle shot. All the shots did was lead us where they wanted us to go. Someone wanted us dead but wanted it to look like an accident."

He reached down a hand to help Caroline up also, careful of the arm that was still sore. "What happens now?" she asked.

"That Mayday you got off to the ranger station will give them a rough idea of where we are."

"Yeah. I've studied the topography maps of Big Bend for weeks, and unfortunately, we are pretty far from any of the ranger stations."

"And none of them have a helicopter or rescue plane just sitting around, I'm sure. Even if they go to the coordinates you gave them in the Mayday, we're still twenty-five miles away from that. It's going to take them a while to find us, even once they have the right equipment to do so."

She tucked a strand of hair behind her ear the way she'd always done when she was thinking. "We don't have any supplies and a storm set is supposed to move in tonight. It's part of the reason I studied the maps so extensively. I wanted to be able to change course as needed based on weather. Where we were before wouldn't have been in the line of the storms, but here…"

"Then let's get out of this ravine in case the storm does come our way. Climbing out of here when it's dry is going to be hard enough." He looked up and around them.

They were in a much more remote and rugged section of the park. No rappelling equipment would be found around here. They would have to take it very slowly and carefully up the steep walls of the ravine. It wouldn't exactly be rock climbing, but it would be close.

Plus, they were overstimulated, hungry and tired. This wasn't going to be fun.

"You ready to do this?" Zane asked as they found the least steep section of the ravine. It was still thirty feet, but at least not at a ninety-degree angle.

Caroline nodded.

"You go up ahead of me." Zane wished he could go first, to help find good footing, but still be under her in case she fell. He couldn't be in two places at once. "Just take it slow. Stop and rest whenever you need to."

He looked up and over at the sky. Zane didn't tell her that time was of the essence—it was getting dark and a storm would be coming in soon. Caroline already knew.

Too slow and they'd be halfway up the ravine and caught in the dark and a dangerous storm. Too fast and one or both of them might fall and seriously injure themselves.

She took her first steps toward the wall, walking at first, then hoisting herself as it became more vertical. They talked through different hand and foot holds, especially as they made it ten, then fifteen feet up the ravine.

A fall now could prove just as deadly as the crash had been. But Caroline never wavered. It was one of the things he'd always admired about her: her ability to focus, set her mind to a task and complete it. It made her one hell of a paramedic.

Not to mention her body had a toned strength to it now that she hadn't had before. She'd always been slender, too skinny in his opinion, but not anymore. A couple of years ago she would've had a difficult time making it up this cliff, even despite her slight size.

But now she had a strength, in both her arms and legs. Even with the injured shoulder, he could tell by the way she was able to stretch, hoist herself up. To use both her arms and legs to lift her body weight. He'd noticed her strength earlier when the repelling gear had given way. Without her grasp on him, keeping herself supported, he wouldn't have been able to get them both down safely.

He could see her lithe muscles moving under her pants and long-sleeve shirt and had to force the thought of what her body would look like now—no clothes at all—out of his head. Now wasn't the time to be doing anything but focusing completely on the task at hand. Not that fantasizing about Caroline was ever appropriate.

About ten feet from the top of the ravine they came to a large crevasse in the rock. An opening big enough for them both. It gave them a chance to rest and sit down.

And realize that the storm was approaching faster than either of them had thought. The temperature had dropped ten degrees since they'd started their climb.

"I think we better stay in here and ride out this storm," Zane said. "Even if we make it up to the top, there's not much shelter up there at all. At least here we'll have a better chance of staying dry."

They needed supplies. Water-resistant material, warmer clothes, sleeping bags. But all those items were still in the packs they'd dropped when they ran. All they had was what Zane had taken out of his hiking pack and left in the small backpack in the plane. In other words, stuff that hadn't been good enough to make first string.

He took the backpack off his shoulders and brought it around to unzip it. He had a second pair of jeans, an extra pair of socks, a sweatshirt and a half-full water bottle. But best of all, a rain poncho.

"Don't guess you have a satellite phone in there?" she asked as he set the items out.

"I wish. Nothing particularly great."

"But added warmth and element protection. So better than nothing."

They decided that Zane would put on the extra pair of jeans under his current hiking pants. It wouldn't be comfortable, but at least it would be an added layer. Caroline slid on his socks which came up to well over her knees and put on the sweatshirt. Her smaller frame would need the warmth more than his would.

She pulled the hood of the sweatshirt up over her head. "At least it's not yellow," she murmured.

Zane had forgotten about that. Caroline's attacker had worn a yellow hoodie. In her pain from the attack, and the way the man had blitzed her, hitting her before she could truly react, she had mistaken a yellow hoodie for blond hair. It had caused the police to arrest the wrong man at first—someone with long, bright blond hair.

Zane wasn't sure exactly what to say. "Are you okay?"

Caroline nodded. "Yeah, believe me, if it will keep me warm, I don't give a damn what color the hoodie is."

"Good. Because that storm is looking uglier every minute." They both looked out at the dark clouds rolling in.

They split the water in the water bottle between the two of them, then Zane set it on the outside of the ledge, where it would catch some rain. He braced it with some of the little rocks around.

Then they slid back as far as they could, about two feet from the outer edge. They lay down nearly on top of one another and cocooned themselves as much as possible in the rain poncho.

And waited for the storm to hit.

Chapter Nine

Hours later, rain pouring all around them in the inky blackness of the night, Caroline lay in Zane's arms.

Somewhere she'd never thought she'd be again.

She wanted to enjoy it, she really did. But huge waves of agony kept pouring over her. Every way she shifted to try to get comfortable on the wet, hard ground of the crevasse just made some other pain worse.

It was everything she could do not to cry. And Caroline was not a crier.

"What if I lie on my back and you ease onto my side. Will that help any?" Zane asked.

"That's just going to cause you to get more wet and cold."

"I'm feeling a little too hot anyway, so why don't we try it?"

She tried to give a small laugh, but it just came out as a puff of air. There was no way Zane was feeling too hot. The weather had dipped another fifteen degrees since nightfall and even in the partial shelter of their overhang they were both still getting wet.

But Zane still moved onto his back, careful to keep the poncho around both their heads and torsos to keep them as dry as possible. Caroline was able to shift some of her weight onto his chest and almost moaned out loud at how good it felt to be more comfortable.

When Zane's arm reached around her and forced her head down on his chest, taking even more of her weight, she couldn't stop the moan.

"That's right. Never let it be said that I don't know how to show the ladies a good time."

Now Caroline did chuckle. He sounded as physically miserable as she felt. "If this is a date, you've definitely got the excitement factor down pat. I'm waiting for a lion to jump up here and attack us, just to finish this day off."

"That's not scheduled for another hour, so you can relax." He shifted a little so more of her weight rested against him. "Are you doing all right? I know your shoulder has to hurt."

"I'd give a lot of money for some ibuprofen right now," she admitted, but didn't want to complain anymore. "How about you?"

"Not comfortable, but considering what we went through? Very grateful we're both alive. I'm sorry your hiking trip was ruined."

"I'm even more sorry that you were right and it ended up being dangerous." She made a sour face.

Zane laughed and pulled her closer. "If it helps, I

don't consider myself to be right. I think having one of federal law enforcement's most wanted criminals personally targeting you counts as extenuating circumstances. Otherwise I think your trip would've been perfectly safe."

"Definitely added some factors I didn't plan for. And by the way, thank you. If you hadn't come out here, I would've been dead a couple times over."

"I wouldn't be too sure of that. I think it's possible that Freihof and his partners followed me. Or that I at least tipped them off as to where you were. It's interesting that you didn't have any trouble at all until after I got here."

"Maybe."

"I can promise you that we're going to catch this guy once we make it back to civilization."

Caroline wondered if Zane knew how much like law enforcement he sounded. Not that she doubted him.

"I believe you. Although it sounds like you might have to get Captain Harris to reinstate you, super cop." She snuggled a little closer. "You always make me feel safe, Zane."

She probably shouldn't admit such a thing; it would make him uncomfortable given how he'd kept himself away from her for so long. It must be the exhaustion or pain getting to her. But it was still the truth.

She couldn't see his face but heard the derision in his laugh. "You're kidding, right?"

"About Harris reinstating you? He would be beside himself with ex—"

"No. About feeling safe with me. Don't joke about that, Caroline. It's not funny."

She shifted her head up slightly, wishing she could see him in the darkness. She might as well tell him the truth; it wasn't like he could be around her any less than he'd been the last year and a half.

"I've always felt safest around you."

"Maybe before you were attacked."

She shrugged painfully. "The attack changed how I saw and thought about pretty much everything. Changed my very DNA, I think, sometimes. But around you is where I have always felt safest."

She could feel tension flood his body. "God damn it, Caroline, you were raped and nearly beaten to death because of me."

Tension flooded her. "What are you talking about? I was attacked because Trumpold was a psychopath."

"Trumpold overheard our conversation, Caro. He knew you had invited me over that night. Knew you would expect *me* to be knocking on your door when I got off my shift. But I decided not to go."

His voice dropped lower.

"We'd been arguing about something that day. For the life of me I can't remember what it was. You were winning, as usual, so I thought I would get the upper hand by not showing up that night."

"Zane, don't—"

His voice rose much louder than needed to be

heard over the storm. "You cannot tell me that you didn't open your door to that sicko because you thought it was me knocking."

She heard the agony in his words and would give anything to be able to tell him that. If only to give him the peace of mind he obviously so desperately searched for. But she couldn't. No matter what she and Zane were or weren't to each other, no matter how tumultuous their relationship, they'd always been honest.

"Yes, I opened the door because I thought it was you," she said softly.

She felt his arm drop from her completely. Felt him almost deflate. Wither.

"How can you say that you feel safe around me after that?" he finally asked. "The night you needed me most I was too busy plotting how to get the upper hand in our relationship."

They lay there for long minutes, silence surrounding them as completely as the storm.

Caroline thought Zane had distanced himself after the attack because he couldn't stomach what had happened to her. That he thought she was too delicate to go back to what their relationship had always been: passionate and sometimes almost violent in its intensity. And maybe that was still true. But she realized now that guilt was the bigger part of what had driven him away all these months.

"Zane, it was Dr. Trumpold. He blitzed his way through the door as soon as it was cracked open. He hit me immediately in the face, and I never saw it was actually him."

"I know." The words were ripped out of Zane's chest. "And you cracked the door in the first place because you thought it was me."

"Maybe." She had to make him understand. To help Zane realize why it had never occurred to her to even partially blame him for what had happened. "Zane, I *knew* Dr. Trumpold. Worked with him almost every day. Yes, I opened the door thinking it was you. *But I would've opened the door to him anyway.*" She spaced out each word to make sure he understood.

It hurt to say them, to even think about that man. She hated that a knock on her door still caused her to blanch and that her first instinct everywhere she went now was to look for danger.

Zane didn't say anything and she didn't really expect him to. He had to process this at his own rate. She didn't blame him; she never had. But she couldn't force him to accept that. They lay there in silence, but eventually Zane's arms found their way back around her, moving in gentle circles on her waist.

"We were fighting that day over which was better, A&M or Austin," she finally said. "I'd insulted your precious Longhorns." She knew that because as she'd come out of the coma, before she'd remembered anything about her attack or felt any of the pain, she'd thought of another point in her argument in the superiority of the Aggies over the Longhorns.

They'd never finished that argument.

She heard Zane curse softly. "I should've known it was about a stupid football team."

"If it hadn't been that, it would've been one of the other hundred topics you and I bickered about on a daily basis. We fought, we made up. We were rough. It's just how we always operated, Zane. It's what worked for us."

Right up until it didn't. Until he stopped fighting. She felt him nod from where she still lay against his chest.

"Our relationship was always so volatile," he whispered softly.

Yes, their passion for each other had been almost violent in its intensity sometimes. She'd loved that they hadn't always made it to the bedroom because they couldn't wait to get at each other. "I remember. Believe me. I remember."

"You say that like it's a good thing."

"Who cares if it was good or bad? It was *us*. And whether people understood it or not, we were good together. Even during our loudest screaming matches."

"But then everything changed." The sadness was pronounced in his tone.

"It didn't have to."

"You told me to stay away from you." He shifted slightly under her. "Not that I blamed you for that. Still don't."

She sighed. "I didn't tell you to stay away from

me. I told you to stop treating me like I was some sort of delicate doll."

"God, Caro, I watched your broken body lying on the ground. I sat by your hospital bed for two days while you were in a coma. And I was the lead detective on the case, so I've seen all the photos of everything else."

She sat up, wanting to be close to him but needing a little distance. At least the rain was starting to back down some.

He continued as if she hadn't moved. "Nobody would've blamed you for never wanting to be around another man ever again. Much less be with me. Not only was it partially my fault…"

She wasn't having any of that. "No. It wasn't."

"But our relationship always bordered on rough anyway. How in the world could I think you would ever want that?"

"So you tried to make it into something it wasn't."

"I wanted to be what you needed." He scrubbed a hand across his face.

"What I needed was someone who didn't treat me like I was never going to be anything but a recovering rape victim! I thought that person was you. It was everything I held on to in the hospital and all through my physical therapy."

"Caro—"

All the feelings and frustrations were flooding out of her now, her own violent storm. She couldn't stop it if she wanted to. "I waited and waited, but you never showed up, Zane. Someone who looked like you did. He held my hand and talked to me. But it was just a pale copy of the original. I needed *you*. I needed *us*. So you're right, when you couldn't provide that, I didn't want you around. I wanted you to treat me like I was *me*."

Zane sat up with her, pulled her closer. She didn't resist. "Caroline."

"But when I told you to go, I never meant for you to stay away forever. I just wanted time to heal. For both of us to heal. Because you needed to just as much as I did."

"You're right. I did." He nodded, still holding her against him.

"But you didn't heal, Zane. You quit the job you loved, the one you were so good at, where you made a difference, and you never came back. You just vanished. You left me too."

"I thought being away from you was the best thing I could do. That you wanted me away. It was the only gift I had left to give."

She wanted to cry. For the past that couldn't be changed. "That was never what I wanted."

He pulled her tighter to his chest, laying them both back down. "I see that now. I didn't handle the situation very well. I know that. My only excuse is that I thought I was doing what you wanted—keeping away from you."

"Maybe we both didn't handle the situation very well." She sighed.

"You had enough to deal with, just getting through every day."

"I would've rather had you there with me."

"I'm here with you now."

She could hear his heartbeat under her cheek. He was with her now. Maybe that was enough.

"You can't treat me like I'm fragile, Zane. Everyone else still does. Like I'm going to crack at any moment. I'm not. I'm strong. That's part of the reason I was hiking out here. To prove I was okay."

"Everyone knows you're strong."

"Do *you*? Do you really, Zane?"

"Yes. I've always known it. But what I saw you do today? Hold it together as the plane was coming down? Direct me with how to get your shoulder back in joint, then climb up a ravine wall? I don't think any sane person could doubt you're strong."

She wanted him to prove it. Prove that he believed it.

Not with words. She knew he could say the words. Knew he even believed the words.

She needed him to show her—to show *both* of them—right now that she wasn't breakable.

The pain in her shoulder didn't matter, the aches and bruises they both had weren't relevant. Caroline wanted to feel alive on the inside. Wanted to feel alive, feel strong and womanly, the way only Zane had ever made her feel.

The storm had slipped by. All they had left was night. Tomorrow the rescue would come.

Tomorrow they'd be going back to real life.

But first she would enjoy Zane the way she had in the past. Before they'd let someone take much more from them than they ever should have given up.

She shrugged the poncho from over her shoulders and threw it to the side. Then she slid up from where she was lying on her side against him so she was straddling his hips. The narrow spacing of the crevasse didn't give her room to sit straight up, so she was forced to hover over him, her breasts pressed against his chest.

"Whatcha doing?" he murmured, his face only inches from hers.

"You've got to prove it."

"Prove that I want you?" His hands gripped her hips and pulled her down harder against him. "I don't think there can be any doubt of that."

"Prove that you really think I'm strong. That you're not afraid I'll break at the least little thing."

"I know you won't."

"Prove it, Zane. Prove that you can still get lost in me. That we can get lost in each other."

His hand reached up and tangled in her hair, bringing her lips down hard against his. His tongue thrust into her mouth and she moaned. Yes. Yes, this was what she wanted.

His teeth nipped at her lips and his arms wrapped more tightly around her.

Their harsh breaths filled the alcove when he broke away after long minutes.

"You want this? Us?" he whispered, pulling her hips more tightly against his.

"Yes. Hard. Now, Zane."

"Fine. But we do it my way."

She cocked an eyebrow. "Your way? Have things changed so much that your way and my way are no longer the same?"

He pulled her down for a punishing kiss. One that bruised her lips.

One that eased something inside her. Revived places in her that had lain dead for too long. She moaned into the kiss and his groan soon joined hers.

"You still have the smartest mouth, that's for sure," he said against her lips. "Here's my deal. I won't hold back. And believe me, Caro, that won't be a problem."

"Good. That's what I want too."

"But…"

She didn't want to hear the but. She covered her lips with his to shut him up. And it worked. For a couple of minutes.

But then his hand wrapped more fully in her hair and pulled her back so he could talk.

"But," he began again as if she hadn't stopped him before. "You're injured from what happened today. So if something starts to hurt too badly, you tell me immediately, okay?"

That she could handle. "Yes."

His fingers eased from where his fist had gripped the roots at her skull. His other hand moved up from her hip and soon both hands were cupping her face, dwarfing her cheeks.

"And if anything else starts to bother you, darkness starts to creep in, anything gets too overwhelming, you have to tell me."

"I thought that you believed I was strong enough to handle it."

"I do. But part of that strength is being willing to speak up if it's too much. You want me to let go? Fine. You're not fragile and I'm not going to treat you like you are. But I have to know, hell, Caro, *you* have to know that at any point a single phrase can stop this."

"Like a safe word?"

"I don't care what you call it, but we've both got to know you've got the means to stop this at any time necessary."

He was right. It was what they should've done years ago. What they should've worked through together from the beginning, but they'd been too stubborn and stupid.

Of course, they'd been that way before the attack too.

"Airplane," she said.

"What?"

"Airplane. That's what I'll say if I'm getting too overwhelmed."

He laughed. "Perfect. At least it's not 'Zane is a jackass.'"

She reached down and kissed him again. "I say that too often for it to be a safe phrase."

"You promise you'll use *airplane* if you need it."

"I promise. You promise not to treat me like I'm going to break."

He kissed her again and her breath whooshed out as he wrapped his arms around her tightly and spun them both so that she was pinned underneath him.

"I promise," he said against her lips. "Tonight we both burn."

Chapter Ten

Waking up with Caroline in his arms was something Zane had given up on ever happening again.

Happening in an alcove in the wilderness twenty-five feet off the ground after their plane had crashed and someone had been shooting at them didn't make it more believable.

The sun was coming up, the worst of the storm had passed and at least rain wasn't pelting them any longer, although Zane knew the low clouds would slow the rescue effort.

Caroline's small body rested, sprawled almost completely on top of his. The low temperatures had demanded they get all their clothes back on before sleeping, but having her this close was almost like skin to skin.

Somewhere in the midst of their lovemaking he'd understood what she'd been trying to tell him. What she wanted from him. From them.

She hadn't wanted him to hold back. But she hadn't been talking just about physically.

Lovemaking between them had always been raw and passionate—rarely ever soft and sweet—and last night hadn't been an exception, as visceral as always. But that wasn't necessarily what Caroline had meant when she'd asked him not to hold back.

She'd wanted him not to hold back *mentally*. Not to let the past take any more away from them than it already had. To not look at her and wonder if she was okay, if something was scaring her, was hurting her, was bringing back memories of the attack.

She wanted him—*them*—to be like it was before those were ever questions in his mind.

She wanted him to want her. Zane wanting Caroline.

And he had.

God, how he had.

And he'd trusted her to tell him if things got to be too much. To use her safe word, airplane. It hadn't been easy to trust her. At first he'd been studying her, pausing, moving with deliberate care to make sure everything was okay with her.

But then he realized that was exactly what she'd been talking about. That was exactly what she *didn't* want.

So he'd let go. Trusted her. Trusted her strength.

Trusted that she would tell him if something didn't work for her. But evidently everything worked for both of them, because once he'd let go, he'd *really* let go and Caroline had been right there with him.

He pulled her closer onto his chest, wincing for her when she moaned slightly in pain even in her sleep. Their escapades last night definitely had not helped all their minor injuries. But neither of them had complained at the time.

He would let Caroline sleep as long as she could, then get the bottle that had collected the water from the storm. It wouldn't be much, but it would be enough.

As soon as the rain cleared, they'd need to make it the rest of the way up the ravine and try to light some sort of signal fire. It would be the most assistance they could offer the rescue plane that would come after them. And Zane knew they would as soon as the storm cleared. Which thankfully wouldn't be too much longer. They had limited food, limited water and no shelter besides this crevasse.

Holding his arms steady around Caroline, staring up at the rock just a couple feet over his head, Zane knew he had to accept that his means of livelihood now lay as charred pieces of metal in the bottom of the ravine. Until he worked out the insurance paperwork and issues, he was without a job.

Which was fine, since he planned for his new full-time job to be protecting Caroline until this Damien Freihof guy was caught. It had nothing to do with not trusting her to take care of herself. Zane would be damned if he would leave her to face this alone.

He held her for the next couple of hours, dozing

himself. When he woke again, the rain had completely stopped.

As much as he didn't want to, it was time to get moving.

"Hey, sleepyhead." He rubbed a hand gently up and down her back. "It's time to get up."

He could tell the exact moment she woke up. Her entire body tensed. Zane wasn't sure what it meant: if she was scared, hurt, embarrassed. All?

He slid his hands off her so she wouldn't feel like anything was trapping her in any way.

"Zane?" she asked hoarsely as she pushed away from his chest, then gasped, he was sure, at the pain it caused her shoulder.

He kept his tone even. "Just me, sweetheart. Hanging out with you here in our little alcove."

He felt her relax as she remembered, although not nearly as relaxed as when she'd slept. "That's right. I remember."

He chuckled. "I hope so. If not, I wasn't doing my job right."

She snuggled a little closer to him like he'd hoped. "I think you did it just fine. But man, I need a toothbrush." Her stomach growled. "And something to eat."

"I have a packet of crackers in my backpack and hopefully the water bottle got filled in the rain. But no toothbrush, sorry."

"Then you definitely won't want to kiss me."

He reached down and tilted her head up until they

were face-to-face. "Believe me, I want to kiss you. No matter what the circumstances, I always want to kiss you." And he did, not giving her a chance to get embarrassed and pull away.

He wanted it to go further. Could tell they both wanted it to go further. But he eased back after a few minutes. They couldn't take a chance on missing the rescue plane when it came by.

"We need to get up to the top," he said as he helped her sit up. "That last part is the steepest, and with your shoulder, it's going to take longer."

He crawled over and got the water bottle, glad to see it was full. They both drank from it, then Zane got the cracker packet out of the backpack. Sharing three peanut butter crackers apiece wasn't going to satisfy hunger very long.

"Do you think they'll find us today?" she asked between bites of cracker.

"Yes. We need to build a fire if we can. Something really smoky will be easier for a pilot to spot than just two people."

"That's good." She nodded. "Because with as wet as the wood is going to be, a smoky fire is going to be the only thing we can get."

They finished their meager meal and began the slow progress of making it up the last ten feet of the ravine wall. Caroline's arm had stiffened while she slept and the swelling from joint trauma had left her hardly able to move it.

To get her up, Zane stood right behind her, supporting her body with his as she hoisted herself up with one arm.

He could tell she was worried and uncomfortable as they made their way up. He didn't blame her. She had to lean all her weight back on him as she moved her one workable arm from one holding point to another. If he lost his grip, they would both fall to almost certain death.

"You're doing great, you know that?"

"Whatever." Her tone was short. He had no doubt if he could see her face she'd be rolling her eyes. Caroline didn't like feeling weak.

But he couldn't see her face because he was behind her, with his body pulled flush against hers. He used that as a method of distracting her, nuzzling his face into her neck.

"I'm in no hurry to get up the wall if it means I can be this close to you."

He felt her ease just slightly.

"You're lucky I have to keep my grip on the rocks or you might be in trouble," he continued. "Do you remember that shower in Houston?"

She'd had a weekend class she was taking to further her paramedic training. Zane had surprised her by meeting her at the hotel and upgrading the room to a special suite. The shower had a rock facade for one of the walls. And Zane had wasted no time getting Caroline's body pressed up against it, not unlike how he had her pressed against the cliff now.

"Yeah, but there I wasn't about to cause us both

to fall to our death because I couldn't get my stupid arm to work properly."

"Trust me, darlin', I'm not going to let either of us fall."

She relaxed back against him more and then climbed the last few feet up to the top. He could tell the effort had taken quite a bit out of her. She needed painkillers, something to reduce the swelling, a full meal and a hot shower.

Zane prayed they had a capable pilot in whoever was working the rescue attempt. These low-lying clouds would make everything more complicated. If the pilot wasn't good at his job, finding them would take a lot longer.

Starting a fire took a long time, since all the wood was wet. Once they did get it started—using every skill Zane had learned as an Eagle Scout and had him swearing he would trade his firstborn child for a set of matches—Caroline was right; it smoked like hell.

But it would be a signal. No one could doubt it was a man-made fire.

Which was good because Caroline's pallor concerned him more with each passing hour. He knew she felt bad when she didn't argue with him about resting rather than helping him gather more firewood. She just nodded.

So when they heard a low-flying plane a couple hours later, Zane's relief was profound. He immediately began fanning the fire with his backpack. Caroline jumped up and waved her good arm. As the plane passed over them, its wings tilted back and forth like a drunk stumbling down the sidewalk. It then flew out of sight.

"Oh no," Caroline cried. "Did they miss us?"

"No, the pilot saw us. That's what the tilting of the wings signified. His best way to signal us."

"But he just left."

"As we found out the hard way yesterday, there's no real place to land around here. Too many trees, and the ravine didn't prove very fruitful as a runway. The pilot will radio in our location. Someone will be here as soon as they can."

Zane was right. A few hours later a park ranger vehicle showed up at their location, complete with food, water and a first aid kit.

After twice the normal dosage of ibuprofen and a relatively full belly, Caroline fell asleep in the back seat of the vehicle as they headed to the ranger station.

"We appreciate the effort you guys put in to finding us," Zane told the park ranger, whose name was Ron Nixon, as they neared the ranger station. They'd kept quiet much of the way to allow Caroline to sleep.

"We're just glad you're both all right. Captain Harris from the Corpus Christi police station had put in a special request to us to keep an eye on Ms. Gill."

"You mean like having her check in with you every few hours?"

Ranger Nixon gave a guilty grimace. "Actually, he asked us to drive out to see her every day. Just make sure she was okay. Told us what had happened to her."

Zane shook his head. Now he understood even more Caroline's insistence on him not holding back, on treating her as if he trusted her to be able to handle the situation put before her.

Because evidently, based on Captain Harris's actions, people were still trying to smother her.

But none of that was Ranger Nixon's fault, so there wasn't any point getting upset with him. He was just doing what had been asked of him. Captain Harris shouldn't have been so quick to share Caroline's personal story. She'd be mortified if she knew.

She just wanted to leave the past behind her. But evidently it was the people she cared about the most who wouldn't let her do that. Zane had been one of those people until last night.

He turned to Nixon. "I think she would've been fine under normal circumstances. No need for anyone to look out for her. This was a case of someone specifically chasing us."

"We're just glad you were able to land the plane. When we got your Mayday, we knew there was trouble based on the location."

"I think *landing* may be too polite of a word for what we did."

Nixon shrugged. "Anything you walk away from is a landing, right?"

Zane smiled. "I'm thankful you could find us this morning. I'm surprised you had a plane out as soon as you did. I thought you might have to bring one in as well as a pilot."

Ranger Nixon pulled the vehicle down the drive to the ranger station. "Normally, we would. But this morning a plane and a couple of pilots showed up on our little landing strip here. Evidently news about your Mayday had gotten around."

"Let me guess. To Captain Harris?" The Corpus Christi PD didn't have an airplane, but Zane wouldn't put it past the man to beg, borrow or steal one to come look for him and Caroline.

"No, not Harris. Much bigger than that."

Nixon didn't need to say any more; the people walking out the door of the ranger station said everything Zane needed to know. Jon Hatton and Lillian Muir from Omega Sector. They'd been the ones who had delivered the plane. One of them had been piloting it, which explained how he and Caroline were found so quickly. There wasn't anyone better in all the country when it came to search and rescue.

As Nixon pulled to a stop, Zane got out of the SUV. He went to shake Jon's hand as the man walked up, but Jon pulled him in for a quick, hard hug instead.

"I'm glad you're okay, brother," Jon murmured. "You and Caroline both."

Hard to believe this was a man Zane had fought with so hard when they'd first met nearly two years ago.

"Me too. She's conked out in the back. Had a dislocated shoulder I had to slip back into joint. That helped, but she was still in a lot of pain."

"Ouch," Lillian murmured.

Zane smiled at the petite woman, a member of the Omega SWAT team. She was damn tough. Zane wouldn't doubt she'd had a dislocated limb at some point in her past. "Thanks for coming, Lil."

"Glad to get away from all the wedding craziness happening at Omega. Steve Drackett got hitched last month. Now this one—" she nudged Jon "—and Sherry. Then Brandon Han and Andrea Gordon are scheduled for February. It's like there's something in the water."

Zane smiled. "By all means, let's get to some more fun stuff, then. Like catching the psychopath who's trying to kill us."

Chapter Eleven

Damien Freihof couldn't have orchestrated this situation any better if he had planned the whole thing himself.

Oh, wait, he *had* planned the whole thing himself, and yep, it had worked exactly how he'd envisioned it.

Damien read again the report given to him from the secretive Mr. Fawkes, a mole inside Omega Sector working with Damien to take the organization down. Damien still didn't know the man's real name, but as long as he kept providing valuable information, he could remain as taciturn as he wanted.

Profiler Jon Hatton and SWAT team member Lillian Muir had rushed down to Texas from Omega Sector headquarters in Colorado to help when they'd heard trouble had found Zane Wales and Caroline Gill. To offer their assistance in any and every way possible, including the use of the search and rescue airplane.

Evidently a Mayday report had come from Zane

Wales's plane to the ranger station. The ranger station had notified the Corpus Christi Police Department, who had notified Omega Sector, who in turn, inadvertently of course, had notified Damien.

Damien didn't much care if Zane Wales and Caroline Gill were dead already or not. If they weren't yet, they would be soon. Besides, they were just a means to an end.

Making Omega Sector pay. Making the members of Omega Sector understand the agony of losing people they love. Damien had already taken the life of one Omega agent, but his plan wasn't to kill off agents one by one.

He wanted to kill the people they *cared* about. Snatch them away. Gut Omega from the inside.

Just like they'd done to him when they'd killed his Natalie. Omega thought the battle had started with him when Damien had gone after SWAT member Ashton Fitzgerald and his lover, Summer Worrall. But it had really started seven years ago with Damien's wife's death in an Omega raid on his home.

Natalie had been his most prized possession. She'd made him the envy of all his friends when she'd married him. He could still picture her beautiful face, her long blond hair, her beautiful blue eyes. The classic American beauty. And she'd been *his*. Only his.

Until Omega took her life.

And now they would pay. One loved one at a time. And then when they knew the agony of love lost,

Damien and the mole, Mr. Fawkes, would destroy Omega for good. Mr. Fawkes had his own political agenda, but Damien didn't care much about that.

A text came to Damien's burner phone. He knew it had to be one of two parties. Either Mr. Fawkes or the Trumpolds, the people who wanted to kill Zane and Caroline.

Mr. Fawkes.

Wales and Gill are still alive after the plane crash. Jon Hatton and Lillian Muir are going with them from Big Bend to CC.

Of course Jon Hatton would go with his friends to Corpus Christi, even with his own wedding coming up next week. After all, Zane and Caroline meant so much to Jon. They meant a lot to many people at Omega Sector.

That was why this entire plan would work. If Omega didn't care, killing the couple in Texas wouldn't make any difference.

Now he had another call to make. To Nicholas Trumpold. Brother of the late Paul Trumpold, the man who had attacked and raped Caroline Gill.

Damien had spent considerable time over the last few weeks convincing Nicholas and his sister, Lisette, that their beloved brother had been framed. That Caroline Gill had lied about the attack and Zane Wales, as an officer of the Corpus Christi PD at the time, had helped frame Paul.

That the police department had been so desperate to make the public think they had put the serial rapist terrorizing the city behind bars they'd looked the other way at evidence that would've exonerated their brother.

None of that was true, of course. Paul Trumpold had been a psychopath intent on hurting women. The hospital photos of the women he'd attacked told a story of sick violence and desire for their humiliation. Trumpold, about to be caught and arrested, had then attacked Jon Hatton and his fiancée, Sherry Mitchell, and nearly killed them both.

But Paul Trumpold's siblings, who had idolized their big brother, had been easily convinced of their brother's innocence.

They'd just wanted to believe it so badly. That he couldn't possibly be the monster he'd been made out to be. Paul had died early in prison and hadn't been around to tell them anything.

The falsified documents Damien had created, making it look as if Caroline and Zane had both lied about the entire situation, had just sealed the deal. From there it hadn't taken long for Damien to convince the Trumpold siblings to get revenge on their brother's behalf.

Of course, they had no idea that them taking revenge would also suit Damien's purpose—it would tear at a piece of Omega.

Omega knew Damien was behind the attacks on their loved ones. Heaven knew, he'd left them enough clues, a whole wall's worth. They even knew about Damien's ability to change his appearance. To make himself look like someone completely different every time he stepped outside. That was what had kept him ahead of law enforcement, and all their facial recognition software, for the past year, since he'd escaped from prison.

Sometimes he went out with no disguises on whatsoever just to mess with them. It was fun to hear about them scurrying around trying to find him like ants.

But now he had a business call to make. He dialed Nicholas Trumpold's number to give them the news that Zane and Caroline were still alive.

"Hello, Damien."

"Where are you, Nicholas?"

"We're outside of Big Bend, if that's what you're worried about. After we sabotaged Wales's plane and led them back to it, we didn't stick around."

"I'm sorry to inform you that Mr. Wales and Ms. Gill made it out of the crash alive." Damien wondered how the other man would take the news.

Silence for a long moment. "Good."

"Good?" That wasn't what Damien had been expecting to hear.

"Lisette and I discussed it. That we had been rash in our decision to kill Wales and Gill and make it look like an accident."

It sounded like the Trumpolds were having second

thoughts. Damien had very little patience for people who deviated from the plan.

Especially when those people were expendable in the overall strategy like the Trumpolds. But Damien kept his patience. "Nicholas—"

"What I mean by that is that if Zane Wales and Caroline Gill had died in either the rappelling accident or the plane crash we set up for them, then the world wouldn't know the truth about our brother. Wouldn't know they lied."

Damien's eyebrow rose. Interesting. "That's true."

"So it's good that they made it out alive. Lisette and I have a new plan."

"And what is that?"

"We're going to get them to confess. To state publicly what they did and clear Paul's name."

There was no way in hell that was ever going to happen, but Damien kept that knowledge to himself. "They've kept it a secret for over eighteen months now. I don't think they're just going to confess."

"Lisette and I have already talked about that. We'll force them to confess."

"Sounds painful." Damien smiled.

"I'm sure it will be."

Evidently Paul hadn't been the only psychopath in the Trumpold family. Sounded like Nicholas was pretty excited about the thought of torturing Zane and Caroline. To get them to confess to something that was completely untrue.

Damien grinned. It was unfortunate for the Texan couple. But it worked just perfectly for him.

FORTY-EIGHT HOURS after Zane's plane had crashed, they made it back to Corpus Christi. Caroline had barely had time to say hello to Jon and Lillian at the ranger station before she was immediately whisked off to the local hospital just outside of Big Bend. An X-ray and MRI had shown that she had no breaks or fractures and that Zane had done a pretty damn good job getting her joint back into the socket.

The doctor gave her a prescription-level painkiller and sent her on her way, calling her very lucky.

Caroline already knew that. Not just because they'd survived the crash, but because of what had happened afterward between her and Zane.

Their lovemaking had been downright fantastic. Not just the physical aspect of it, although that had been awesome too, but the fact that for the first time since the attack Caroline had just felt *normal*.

Maybe not actually normal, since they'd been in an overhang on the middle of a cliff surrounded by a storm after surviving a plane crash. But normal as in Caroline and Zane.

Not rape survivor Caroline. Just *Caroline*.

And it had felt amazing.

In all possible ways.

She knew it didn't solve all the problems, particularly the fact that they had someone trying to kill them. But damned if Caroline didn't feel better than she had in months.

Zane had made love to her like he used to. Like he wasn't afraid she would break or run screaming. She peeked over at him from where she sat in the passenger's seat now, his strong arms gripping the steering wheel, easing them through Corpus Christi traffic. They'd just come from the police station.

"Captain Harris looked pretty giddy to have you back." She couldn't help but tease him. They'd dropped Jon and Lillian at the department so Jon could brief Harris and the other officers about what was going on. Harris, once he'd heard about Zane's plane, had told him the only logical thing—given the circumstances—was for Zane to be reinstated as law enforcement.

Kill two birds with one stone: Zane needed temporary employment, and Corpus Christi needed one of their best detectives back on the job.

Zane grimaced. "I thought he might actually break out into a jig when I said I would come back temporarily."

"He never filled your detective position, you know. Hemmed and hawed about budget cuts, but we all knew he was hoping you would return."

She saw his fingers tighten on the steering wheel. "I don't think Harris or anybody else should put too much faith in me. Not only am I rusty, I wasn't at the top of my game when I left."

Caroline studied him. She'd lost so much in the

attack, but Zane had lost a lot too. The difference had been that her wounds were visible and she'd therefore gotten all the help and support she'd needed.

Had Zane gotten any help or support? Would he even have accepted it if anyone offered? Knowing him, probably not.

"Airplane," she said to him.

"What?" He glanced at her before looking back at the road. "Wait. Is there a reason why you're using your safe word? Are you okay?"

"No, I'm fine. But you need a safe word. Have you ever thought of that?"

"What?"

"Okay, maybe not a safe word. But you know how I had to almost force you into treating me normally in the ravine? When we—" She floundered, unable to get the words out, suddenly feeling a little embarrassed.

He glanced at her again, eyebrow raised. "Had incredibly awesome sex?" He reached out and grabbed her hand, entwining their fingers.

She flushed but grinned. "Yes. That. It wasn't until I demanded you treat me normally that you did it."

"Okay, I still don't understand what this has to do with me needing a safe word."

"You don't need a safe word. But you do need to force yourself to start treating *you* normally."

He glanced at her with one eyebrow raised. "I'm pretty sure I don't know what you're talking about."

But he did. She knew he did. "I'm pretty sure you

do. Enough, Zane. Just like you had to stop treating me like I was broken, you have to stop treating yourself that way."

He let go of her hand, making it look like he needed both of his on the wheel, but she knew him well enough to know that he didn't like to think she might be right.

"You have to admit what you lost in the attack, Zane."

"I lost you."

"You lost more than that. You lost your faith in yourself. Your confidence as a law enforcement officer. Things were taken from *you* in my attack too."

Zane scoffed. "Oh, boo-hoo. Compared to what you lost, who gives a rat's ass what I lost."

"It's not a damn competition, Zane. Nobody gets a trophy for losing the most." Her voice was rising. His was too.

But she didn't mind fighting with him. It was just more proof that he wasn't holding back.

"I know that." He slid his fingers through his hair in a frustrated gesture. "But I also know that what I lost was nothing compared to what you did."

"And I had people lining up down the block to help me. To talk to me. Do you know that Grace Parker, the top psychiatrist at Omega Sector, has been counseling me?"

"No." He glanced at her again. "I assumed you had someone you talked to, but I didn't know it was someone with Omega."

"She's the best there is. I love her."

"I'm glad you have someone. That's important in a situation like this."

"Exactly." She paused for just a minute. "Who do you have, Zane? Who have you talked to?"

He didn't answer, just stared out the windshield.

"This was too big to tackle on our own. For either of us," she said quietly. "Even now."

"Well, I'm fine. People have different ways of coping. You talked to a shrink. I—"

"Ran away from a job you loved and moved to the outskirts of town so you would never have to run into me or any of your colleagues unless you wanted to." Now it was her turn to raise an eyebrow at him.

"Just leave it alone, Caroline. I did what I thought I had to do."

Knowing what he thought, how he blamed himself for her attack, Caroline understood that. But it was time for a change.

"Do you still feel like it's what you have to do? Even after what happened between us at Big Bend?"

"I feel like right now we need to focus on keeping Damien Freihof and whoever he's working with from carrying out their plans to kill us. The rest can wait."

"You're avoiding, Zane."

"I'm working on keeping us safe."

Caroline had meant to tell him where her new town house was, the one she'd moved into just a couple of months ago. But she realized Zane already knew.

"You know where I live." Her tone was accusatory.

"Yes."

"I only moved there six weeks ago."

He shrugged. "I knew when you moved. I've always known. I knew when you moved to the place before that. And the other. I knew when you moved out of your parents' house. Although I wasn't surprised at that."

"I couldn't live there anymore. None of us ever wanted to set foot there again. They sold it."

"I don't blame you. Don't blame them."

"Then the other places... I just had a hard time. Tried living with a roommate, and that didn't work. Moved on my own. Tried a second-floor apartment. Just trying different things to see what worked for me."

"And this new place?"

"I've come to discover it's not really the place that makes that much of a difference. It's my frame of mind. Sometimes I have no problem for days or even weeks. But then sometimes..." Caroline shrugged. "The other night when we saw each other at the Silver Eagle, I was there because I couldn't force myself to go into my town house alone."

"I'm sorry."

"I have good days and I have bad days. That would be true for you too if you came back to law enforcement, you know. You would have some bad days. But some would be good."

"Give it a rest, Caro. I'm already temporarily reinstated."

"Maybe I miss your white hat."

"You hated that hat. Knocked it off my head every chance you got."

Only so she could run her fingers through his hair, but she didn't have to tell him that. "Well, now I miss it."

He pulled up to her town house. "I'm not leaving you here, by the way."

"I can take care of myself."

"That's great. You can take care of yourself with me at your side. Keys."

She rolled her eyes. "Whatever. I just want to get into some different clothes. We can fight about this later."

She tossed him the keys and he opened the truck door before turning back to her. "Wait here. Just in case."

He drew his gun from his belt holster and moved into the town house. Just a couple minutes later he came back out.

"Okay, looks like we're clear."

Entering her town house was quite a bit easier with Zane by her side, she had to admit. But even then she felt compelled to do her normal safety routine as soon as she walked in.

She looked at him. "Um, airplane."

He immediately stepped closer, face concerned. "What's going on? How can I help?"

She wanted to kiss him for knowing the perfect

thing to say without even thinking about it. She knew he took her seriously without wanting to fix it himself.

"I have a process. Something I do every time I come home. I need to do that now, if it's okay."

He looked relieved. "Sure."

"It's a little weird."

"Does it involve you getting naked and dancing in the middle of the living room?"

She smiled. "No, sorry."

"Damn it. Whatever, then. Do your boring little weird thing."

Caroline began walking around the living room, running her fingers along the bottom of each of the windowsills where they met the apron—the little ledge sticking out. By the time she got to the third one she knew Zane had to wonder what exactly she was doing, but he waited patiently.

After she'd checked all the windows she walked to the back door and crouched down. She looked toward the bottom of the door and froze at what she saw. "Zane?"

"Yeah?" He was to her in a second. "What's going on?"

"Someone has been in my town house."

Chapter Twelve

Zane immediately had his sidearm out again. He'd already checked her small place pretty thoroughly.

"There's no one in here now, that's for sure. How do you know someone has been in here?"

She showed him a piece of clear tape she'd put at the bottom of her back door. Immediately he realized how it worked. The tape was unnoticeable when the door was closed, covering both the door and frame. But if the door opened, the tape came unstuck from the door frame.

Very simple but very effective. It was what she had been checking for at each of her windows also.

"I always have this on the back door and windows." She grimaced. "It's one of the coping mechanisms Dr. Parker and I came up with."

He put his gun away. "To know if someone has been in the house?"

"About eight months after the attack I started waking up at night terrified someone was in the house with me. That was the second time I moved into a place that had as few windows as possible." She shrugged. "The tape was a simple method that allowed me to know for sure, to convince my terrorized mind at three o'clock in the morning that no one could possibly be inside."

He reached over and yanked her into his arms, thankful when she didn't stiffen or pull away, as emotion nearly overwhelmed him. Her words broke his heart and yet made him so damn proud of her at the same time.

"I think it's brilliant if you ask me."

He felt her good shoulder shrug slightly. "At first I considered myself a coward. I could understand and condone moving out of my parents' beach house, where the attack happened. But moving to the second place, with less windows, just seemed cowardly."

"But it wasn't."

"No. It took me a while to figure that out. Recovery is not a straight line. It's sometimes one step forward and half a mile back. Setbacks are part of the process."

Zane realized *he* should have been part of her process too. Maybe he could've helped her through some of this if he'd chosen to really listen to her needs rather than give her what *he* thought she needed.

Maybe the tape still would've been necessary. But maybe knowing he was there would've been enough.

"Hey, in the now, Wales."

"What?"

"Whatever it is that has you all stiff? Let it go. We

can't change the past. We can only change what we choose to do today."

She was right. And today, right now, involved the fact that someone had been inside her town house. He reluctantly let her go.

"I assume you didn't ask anyone to water plants or bring in your mail while you were gone?"

"No. No plants. And I had asked the post office to hold my mail."

"It could be innocent. Smoke detector malfunctioned and the landlord came in. Something like that."

But after someone had tried to kill them multiple times, neither of them actually believed that was the case. And since he hadn't planned on leaving her alone anyway, he might as well take her with him instead.

"Let's get what you need. Try to touch as little as possible. I'll send the CSI team in here to see if we can get any prints. Since the perp didn't think you'd know he was in here at all, maybe he didn't wear gloves."

"I hadn't thought of that. I have a landline if you want to call it in." They'd both lost their phones at Big Bend.

"Really? Most people don't anymore. Just use their cell phones."

She shrugged. "Another coping mechanism. Knowing I would always have two different ways of calling for help if needed."

"Smart again."

"One of the first things Dr. Parker and I discussed was that I didn't need to apologize for how I chose to survive. I wasn't doing drugs. Wasn't drinking obsessively or breaking any laws. So anything I did to help cope wasn't anything to be ashamed of."

He kissed her forehead. "Damn straight."

He helped her gather a couple of changes of clothes and toiletries.

"Where are we going?"

"We'll go to my place. But first things first, we've got to get both our phones replaced."

They left Caroline's town house and took care of the tedious job of getting new phones. By that time Caroline was looking pretty tired and Zane was feeling it too. They needed a good night's sleep to face what was ahead.

Not to mention he very much looked forward to having Caroline in an actual bed.

But when they arrived at Zane's house, he didn't need a broken piece of tape on the door to know someone had been in his place.

Someone had completely trashed it.

Once he got the door open and saw the damage, he immediately drew his weapon. "Caro, go wait outside."

"What? What is it?"

"Someone's been in here."

"I'll call Captain Harris."

"Call Jon and Lillian too."

Zane's house on the outskirts of town wasn't much. Two bedrooms, one bath. He'd basically rented it because of its proximity to the airfield he spent so much time at with his business. And because he hadn't been able to force himself to live at the house he'd bought.

Whatever care the intruders had taken at Caroline's house to make sure they would go unnoticed, they'd done the opposite here. Furniture was overturned, dishes broken, contents of drawers strewn everywhere.

Someone had been pissed off when they did this.

"Jon and Lillian are on their way. ETA about ten minutes. Captain Harris said he would have the crime lab techs come over here as soon as they're done with my town house."

"Okay."

"Is it all right for me to come in or should I stay outside?"

In most cases Zane would have people wait outside. Less chance of contaminating possible evidence. But he didn't want Caroline out there exposed in case the person who did this wasn't done with their little temper tantrum.

"Do you mind coming in but just staying by the door?" They'd still be able to see and hear each other.

"Sure."

He heard Caroline's low whistle when she saw the state of his house. "Unless your housekeeping skills took a sharp turn for the worse after we broke up, someone was really angry in here."

Zane nodded. "Generally speaking, destruction of

this magnitude would suggest that the perp knows me personally. Has a personally directed anger toward me."

"You and the contents of your fridge." She pointed toward the kitchen, where everything that had been in his refrigerator now lay all over the floor.

"Sometimes someone can be searching for something and when they can't find it they go into a rage. But this is extreme even for that."

"And what would someone have been looking for in your house?"

"I have no idea. And especially Damien Freihof. I didn't even know who he was until Jon told me about him."

"Me neither. And I can't figure out what he has to do with us."

"Only that we have ties to Omega. That seems to be it." Zane looked through his bedroom and the bathroom—same sort of destruction, no discernible pattern—before coming back out to the kitchen.

"Did the same person who broke into my house do this to yours?" Caroline asked from where she still stood just inside the door.

"Probably."

"Why were they so destructive here but not at my place?"

He stood in the middle of the room, turning so he could see everything, trying to look at it from a detached, professional opinion.

"Either they escalated in anger, maybe starting

with something at your place, then ending it here. Or…" He trailed off, not liking where his thoughts were heading.

"What?"

"Or they've been after me from the beginning and I led them straight to you at Big Bend."

"I thought Jon said both our names were found in whatever clues Damien Freihof left for Omega."

"Yes, but you can't deny that there's definitely an anger here that wasn't present at your house."

"But maybe they came here first."

Zane had to admit that could be true. There were too many unknown variables. But one thing would give him some information: the food.

He walked into the kitchen and bent down to where the half gallon of milk had been thrown onto the ground and spilled.

He smelled it.

"I'm SWAT and don't really do much detective work, but I'm going to go with my gut on this one and say that's milk," Lillian said from the door.

Zane got back up from the ground. "Hey, guys."

"Wow, they really did a number on this place," Jon said, pulling on a pair of gloves.

"Yeah. Forensics team is on their way over," Zane told him. Lillian stayed near Caroline at the door. "The milk has no smell."

"None? Not the least bit of souring?"

"No. As a matter of fact, it's still a little cool."

Both men now had their hands near their sidearms.

It was warm enough in Zane's house that milk that had been out for a day or two would've at least been room temperature. Not cool.

This had happened recently. Whoever had broken into Zane's house had done it in the last few hours.

Jon crouched down next to Zane to touch the milk himself.

"Whoever it was could've been here waiting to ambush you or figured you would both be here," Jon said in a volume that wouldn't carry to the door.

Zane glanced over to where Lillian and Caroline were talking to each other. "Yeah, if we hadn't had to replace our phones, we would've been here hours ago. I've got to take Caroline somewhere safe."

"Hotel?"

"No. I have someplace else in mind." A place he'd never planned to tell Caroline about. But it would be much more comfortable than a hotel. "It will be better, since we don't know how long it will take to catch Freihof and his goons."

"About that." Jon grimaced.

"What?"

"We had a confirmed sighting of Freihof in Colorado Springs at the same time your trouble was happening in Big Bend. I mean obvious. Freihof is pretty brilliant when it comes to disguises and he definitely wanted to make sure we knew it was him and we knew he was in Colorado."

"So whoever tried to kill us wasn't him."

Jon shrugged. "He wasn't physically present in

Texas is all I'm saying. The last person who came after someone at Omega wasn't actually Freihof—it was someone he had convinced needed to take revenge."

Jon explained about SWAT member Ashton Fitzgerald and how he'd been hunted down by Curtis Harper, the son of a man who'd been killed in an Omega SWAT raid years ago. Freihof had told Harper he would help the man get his revenge.

Harper had nearly died in the process, since Freihof hadn't mentioned that he would blow up Harper along with any nearby Omega agents.

"Lillian is here, if needed, as a sort of protection duty for Caroline. I thought Caroline might be more comfortable with a woman," Jon continued. "If you weren't around."

And there it was again. The good intentions Caroline spoke about. People—even her best friend's fiancé—wanting to protect her, but it made her feel weak, breakable.

But on the other hand, Zane knew what Lillian could do. Could kill a man with her tiny bare hands and not break a sweat. As far as protection detail went, very few could beat Lillian Muir, man or woman. And right now, no matter why Lillian was the one chosen, they needed all the help they could get.

"So if Freihof didn't do it, then he's either hired someone to come after us or has found someone from my past. I've arrested a lot of people. Quite a few who would be pretty pissed off. A couple who it wouldn't take much to talk into coming after me."

Both men stood. "And honestly, brother, it wouldn't take very much observation to realize that the best way to get to you, to cause you pain, is through that lady over there." Jon pointed at Caroline.

"I've got to keep her safe, Jon. I can't stand the thought of anything happening to her. Not again."

"I know. You get her someplace safe, away from her house or here. And until we know more, telling as few people as possible where that place is might be a good idea. Lillian and I will wait for the crime scene team here."

Zane nodded. "Thanks, Jon. I'll be in touch to-morrow."

Jon slapped him gently on the shoulder as Zane turned toward Caroline.

He would keep her safe no matter what. Knew where it was that he would take her. Even if it meant giving up the secret he never meant to share with anyone. Especially her.

Chapter Thirteen

"Zane, where are we going?"

They'd been driving around in his truck for nearly an hour now. Every time she thought she knew where they were headed, Zane would make a sudden turn, leading them to another part of town.

Not that Caroline minded riding around in his truck like old times, but Zane was becoming more tense as they drove.

"I don't think either my house or yours is safe. As a matter of fact, Jon and I both feel whoever broke in did it after the attempt on our lives at Big Bend, not before. Maybe even earlier today."

Suddenly the danger seemed even closer and she understood why Zane was driving them around. He was making sure no one was following them. That would also explain his tension.

"So a hotel? Somewhere to hang out?" They needed rest. She needed rest. She needed to feel Zane's arms around her again.

She realized they were headed toward the beach,

maybe a hotel nearby. She hadn't been there in a long time. She sighed. Yet another thing she'd allowed to be taken from her in the attack. But it would be different with Zane with her.

Zane's presence always made everything different.

Zane didn't answer her question, and she didn't push. He obviously had a plan and she trusted him. It wasn't long before they pulled up to a house a couple blocks from the oceanfront, and only a couple of neighborhoods over from where her parents' house used to be.

There weren't any hotels in this area of the beach. Just houses.

"Where are we going? There aren't any hotels here."

"We're not staying at a hotel."

She looked around, unable to decide if this area should make her uncomfortable or not. It wasn't anything at the beach that had hurt her. The man who had caused her such pain was dead.

"A safe house? Something of the department's?"

She didn't think they would have an oceanfront safe house, but crazier things had happened.

"No, it's not the department's. But it is safe."

They pulled into the drive of a small house, about a block and a half from the actual waterfront. Like many of the houses so close to the ocean, there was no full bottom floor. It was built on glorified stilts to keep the water from doing much damage during hurricane season. The entire living area started on the second floor. This allowed Zane to pull his truck all the way under the house to park.

They both got out and Zane grabbed their duffel bags from the cab behind his seat. He led her up the stairs and pulled out a key on his normal key ring and unlocked the door, holding it open for her, and walking in behind her.

She looked around, taking in the open floor plan with the cozy living room—complete with couch and love seat—opening up into the kitchen. From first glance there looked to be three bedrooms, two on one end of the living room, a master bedroom on the other side.

Zane wasn't looking around at all, obviously familiar with the house and its layout.

"What is this, a rental? A friend's place?"

He set the bags down. "No. Actually, I own it."

She spun to stare at him. "You own a house at the beach." She couldn't help but laugh. "You hate the beach. I used to have to drag you here whenever I wanted to go. What, did you buy it as an investment property or something?"

"Something like that."

"I guess it's hard to rent it out during the winter."

Zane just shrugged, walking over to get a bottle of water out of the refrigerator. Except, why would he know there was water in the fridge? He shouldn't be that familiar with what was on the inside of the rental property.

There was something Zane wasn't telling her.

"Does anyone know we're here?"

"I gave Jon and Lillian the address, but not anybody from the department. Why?"

She walked over and opened the refrigerator. It didn't have a lot of stuff in it, but neither was it empty. "I just wondered if you had someone come stock the house for us."

"No, I wanted to keep our whereabouts as tightly guarded as possible."

She turned around to face him, crossing her arms over her chest. "You don't rent this place out, or at least you haven't for a while."

Zane took a chug of his water. "No. You're right. I don't rent it out."

"Do you live here too?" Caroline couldn't figure out what piece of the puzzle she was missing. "Two houses or something?"

"No. I've slept here occasionally when I haven't wanted to drive all the way back out to my house. But, no, I don't live here."

"So let me see if I understand. You own a pretty nice beach cottage. It would make a great place to live, but you don't live here. It would also make a great rental property, but you don't rent it out."

"Just leave it alone, Caroline."

She shook her head. "Why? What is there to leave alone? It's weird, Zane. And not very financially smart."

"Yeah, I'm well aware of the fact that a mortgage and a separate rent payment every month, even though my place near the airfield is pretty negligible in terms of rent, is not the best plan."

This was ridiculous. "Then why the hell are you doing it? Move here."

"I can't. Like you said, I don't like the beach."

She rolled her eyes. "Then sell or rent this place, for heaven's sake."

"I can't do that, either."

"Why the hell not?" Her volume was going up, but she couldn't help it.

His fist slammed down against the kitchen island. "I bought this place for you, okay? For us."

"What?" She reared back a step.

The anger in his voice had disappeared. "I closed on this house two weeks before you were attacked. I had planned on asking you to move into it with me. But then..."

But then everything changed.

She took a step closer, but it felt like a chasm separated them rather than one small kitchen. "You never told me. Even after."

"There was never a good time. First you were in recovery. Then you wanted nothing to do with the beach. Then..." He trailed off, turning away and walking over to the massive doors that led out to the deck. He opened them and glanced back at her over his shoulder. "Then you wanted nothing to do with me."

Caroline watched as he walked outside, bracing

his forearms on the rail of the deck, looking out at the view of the ocean the house afforded.

She looked at the house with new eyes. He'd bought this for *them*.

It was perfect, she realized. Would've been just what she would've wanted to start a life together with Zane.

She wanted to yell, to scream out her pain. To find that she'd lost even more than she'd ever known was almost too much to bear.

She'd already lost so much. They both had.

She looked at Zane standing out on the deck, staring at the sea. Standing on the deck he'd known she would love. Hell, she already did and she hadn't stepped foot out there yet.

Could she walk out there to Zane right now, on the deck that should've been theirs, and try to make everything right? To make their relationship what it was?

No, she couldn't. Too much time had passed. For both of them. Things were too different. Their relationship could never be what it once was.

But that didn't mean it had to be nothing.

She'd spent a lot of time with Dr. Parker in those first few months just trying to get things back to standard, to ordinary. Except Caroline had no idea what ordinary was. She and Dr. Parker had worked long and hard on establishing a new baseline of normal. Of accepting that things would never go back to the way they were, but that didn't mean you were never okay again.

She and Zane had to establish a new baseline of normal.

Starting right now.

She began walking toward him just as he turned to look at her. They were in sync, the way they'd always been. She stepped out onto the deck and he reached his hand out toward her. Neither of them said anything, just held on to one another's hand.

Finally, Zane pulled Caroline against his chest as he leaned back on the railing. She wrapped her arms around his trim waist, hooking her thumbs into the back belt loops of his jeans. The beat of his heart under her ear reassured her of her safety much more than the waist holster she'd felt briefly as she'd slipped her arms around him.

She wished she could just stay against him forever.

But her phone chirped obnoxiously from her pocket.

"Text?" he asked.

"Yes," she murmured, her mouth half against his shirt. "Just ignore it."

"It might be Jon or the precinct." He slipped his fingers into her pocket to pull it out. "Or, God forbid, your parents."

Caroline smiled, letting him read the text. Her parents hadn't ever really liked Zane. Or at least hadn't liked how volatile their relationship was. But they would have no idea he was around, so she doubted it would be anything about Zane.

But she felt him stiffen beneath her. "What the hell, Caroline?"

"What?"

He spun the phone around so she could read the message.

You're a liar and you deserve everything you've got coming to you. Don't think you've escaped.

Caroline grabbed the phone. "Oh yeah. I forgot about these stupid texts. I keep meaning to ask someone how to block this number."

"How long have you been getting them?"

"I don't know." She pulled away, the peace she'd known just a few moments before, gone. "A week? Why are you getting all angry? It's just a wrong number."

"A wrong number? Someone is trying to kill you, Caroline. You should've told me about this. They've got to be connected."

"I didn't think about it, okay? And then I didn't have my phone, so I didn't get any messages."

She looked up at him, ready to blast into him again, but realized there was something else. "What? What aren't you telling me?"

He reached into his pocket and held out his phone so she could see the message that had just arrived for him.

What you hid will come to light. Soon the whole world will know.

She grabbed the phone out of his hand. "What? Is this your first message?"

"No. Like you, they've been coming for a week."

"Zane—"

He took her hand and led her inside. "Yeah, I know. This means we're both being targeted. We've got to get these phones to the station, see what info the tech department can get from them."

"Do you think it's someone local?"

"I don't know. But I plan to find out."

Chapter Fourteen

"Okay, I know this is a hard question, but I need honesty from both you guys," Jon said to them as they sat around the table in the Corpus Christi PD conference room.

They'd brought the phones back last night and left them for tech—happy to get the overtime—to sort through. Zane had let Jon and Lillian know about the texts but then had explained they were going back home.

Home. Zane didn't let himself think too much about that. For nearly two years he hadn't let himself think about the beach cottage and what it represented and how he hadn't been able to let it go. A shrink would have a field day with that one. Maybe that was why he'd never gone to talk to anyone about his feelings.

But taking Caroline home with him, despite the danger, had just felt right. And getting her into a bed with him and making love, slowly, softly—such a different pace for them—had definitely felt right.

But now the time for tenderness was over. It was time to do whatever was necessary to find who was targeting them and make sure Caroline was safe again.

"Despite what the texts imply, Jon, I don't think either Caroline or I have anything to hide."

Jon leaned back in his chair. "I don't doubt that. But I thought we should start with the opening. If either of you took up shoplifting or ran over your neighbor's cat and buried it in your yard, now is the time to come clean with that."

It was good to have Jon here with them. It eased some of the pressure. He knew them, they didn't have to go through the awkward stages of building up trust. Jon wanted to protect Caroline and stop whoever was behind this almost as much as Zane did. After all, Caroline was the best friend of Jon's bride-to-be. The wedding was scheduled for this weekend.

"All right," Caroline said. "I'll admit, the first bridesmaid dress your fiancée picked out? I threatened to kill her if she went with that one. Pretty sure I said it publicly."

Jon chuckled. "The powder blue one?"

Caroline rolled her eyes. "For an artist, she had some pretty big missteps there for a while. Fortunately, she finally picked a great one and I didn't have to kill her."

Jon smiled. "But seriously. Zane, any corners you cut as you got your business started? Caroline, any accidents where maybe you covered a bad call by telling a lie?"

Zane could see both he and Caroline becoming defensive. Nobody liked to have their integrity questioned.

Jon held out a hand. "Listen, you guys are like family to me. And I would personally vouch for both of you without question. But if you've got something you need to get off your chest, now is the time."

"I've got nothing, Jon." Caroline sat up taller in her seat as she said it. "There was a drunk who was threatening to get me fired a few days ago at an accident scene, since I wouldn't stay and look at his dislocated pinkie when I had a bunch of other people around me with serious injuries. But that's the only incident I can recall in the recent past. Since the attack, I've basically just spent most of my time surviving and coming to grips with reality."

Jon nodded, then turned to Zane. "You? I remember you had quite the hot temper when we worked together nearly two years ago."

Zane shrugged. "Still do. But I've kept to myself. Hell, I can't even remember having a real conversation with anyone outside my friends on the force for the past six months."

"Okay." Jon put both hands down on the desk. Obviously, he believed them and wasn't going to belabor the point. "Then let's talk about what the tech folks found out about the texts to your phones."

Jon pulled out papers and handed Zane and Caroline both copies. "Here's a list of all the texts that both of you received and the day and time they were sent."

"They were all sent close to the same time to both of us," Caroline pointed out.

"Yes." Jon nodded. "And they all came from the same phone. Not listed as registered to anyone, unfortunately."

Zane looked at the list of messages. There had been fourteen sent over the last eight days. Each one called Caroline a liar in some way and accused Zane of hiding something.

"So is this a dead end?" he asked Jon.

"We've got Omega looking into it. They've got more sophisticated technology to pull data from the phones. Maybe they can get something Corpus Christi couldn't."

"Okay." Zane sat back in his chair. "Did the CSI crew find anything at my house? Fingerprints?"

He appreciated that Jon had been keeping an eye on this so that Zane and Caroline could get a night of much-needed rest.

"Nothing usable. I stayed with them to see if I could figure out any patterns. See what the perp's overall plan was. But it honestly just looked like a fit of rage to me."

One of the CSI personnel came rushing into the room. "Detective Wales, Agent Hatton, we have something you need to see in the lab."

Zane grabbed Caroline's hand and they rushed

with Jon down the hall to the lab. They were met by Susan McGuinness, head of the CCPD crime lab.

"Zane, good to have you back here. We've missed you."

"Thanks, Susan. What's going on? Did you find something at my house?"

"No, actually, we found something at Caroline's house."

"Mine?" Caroline asked. "There wasn't any damage at my house."

"If it wasn't for Caroline's trick with a piece of tape, we wouldn't have known anyone was in there at all."

Susan nodded. "No doubt that's what the person who broke in wanted."

"Tell me you found a fingerprint, Susan."

"Would that be enough to get you to agree to return to the force full-time?" the older woman asked.

Zane could feel Caroline's smile and her eyes on him. He just shrugged. "Maybe."

"Well, unfortunately, it's not a fingerprint we found. But it is something much more interesting."

"What?" He, Jon and Caroline all asked at the same time.

"Transmitting devices. Hidden in two of Caroline's lamps."

Of all the things Jon was expecting to hear, this didn't even make the list. "Are you serious?"

"It wasn't us who found them, actually. It was that other Omega Sector agent. The lady," Susan said.

Jon looked closer at the bugs. "Lillian Muir. She's actually SWAT, not an investigator."

"Well, she was the one who found the bugs after we'd already left."

Jon nodded. "She and I agreed to split up. This morning we wanted to make sure no one was returning to the scene of the crime looking for either of you. She probably went inside to check."

"When she found something unusual, she went out and called us," Susan continued. "Smart on her part. We were able to figure out they were transmitting devices and that they were still actively transmitting."

Zane turned to Caroline and Jon. "That was probably why they trashed my house. To keep us focused over there instead of at your house, Caro. I never even thought to look for transmitting devices."

She shrugged. "I wouldn't have, either."

Jon turned back to the crime lab director. "Can we get any information from the devices? Anything specific about them?"

Lillian walked through the door. "You guys hear about the bugs at Caroline's house?"

"Susan was just telling us," Zane responded. "We're trying to figure out if there's anything usable in the bugs."

Susan looked over at Lillian. "We don't know."

"When will you know?" Zane asked.

"Well." Lillian smiled. "The lab doesn't know anything about the devices because I talked them into leaving them functional at Caroline's town house."

Caroline's eyes flew to Zane's, distress clear, but Zane already knew what Lillian was thinking. "So we can set a trap," he said.

"Yep." Lilian nodded. "I was very careful not to report finding the bugs while I was inside the house, and I made sure none of the nerds—" she turned to Susan "—no offense, said anything while we were inside."

"None taken," Susan responded. "It's a solid plan."

"So the perp doesn't know we know," Zane said, reaching for Caroline's hand. "This could be the break we need."

Caroline still didn't look convinced. "So we, what, go back to my house and give who is listening false information?"

Zane nodded. "Sort of. We can tell them whatever we want. They've got no reason not to believe it."

"We'll fabricate a situation where you guys are away from the department," Jon said. "Dinner or a walk or something."

"I don't want to take a chance with Caroline."

"Zane—"

He cupped her cheek with his hand. "It has nothing to do with not trusting you or thinking you can't handle yourself. I swear to you I would say this about any civilian. You don't have the training to be used as bait. It's too dangerous."

"Caroline, Zane's right," Lillian said. "It's a much better plan to let me wear a wavy brown wig and pose as you. We're roughly the same build. Until someone got right up on us, they wouldn't know it wasn't you."

Jon smiled kindly. "And once the perp is close enough to know the difference, we'll have officers waiting to arrest him."

"How do we know the guy won't just shoot? He was shooting at us at Big Bend," Caroline pointed out.

Zane could see her point. "He was trying to make our deaths look like an accident. Shooting us won't give him that."

"But he could decide to take his chances," Lillian pointed out. "We'll have to give a situation where you're vulnerable, but long-range shooting isn't an option."

Zane nodded. There were a lot of options. They just needed to figure out the best one. He didn't mind putting himself in danger if it meant catching the person intent on hurting Caroline.

"I don't like you setting yourself up," Caroline looked up at him with her big green eyes. "The same way you don't want me to do it, I don't want you to, either."

He smiled gently. "If I'm law enforcement, it's what I do."

She kissed the palm of his hand cupping her cheek. "Law enforcement or not, you watch your back."

"I won't have to. I've got the best doing that for me."

THEY DIDN'T WASTE any time putting their plan into action, knowing every moment they didn't make a move gave the killer more time to scheme.

So a few hours later Caroline found herself and Zane back at her town house, playing out a script they'd already formulated at the station.

"I just need a break, Zane," Caroline said as they walked in the front door. "This was supposed to be my vacation."

"It's not my fault someone is trying to kill you," Zane said, playing his part. "It's just not safe for you to go anywhere alone right now."

"I spent the entire day at the police station. I don't like the station. You know that. It brings back bad memories." Those words didn't require much acting. She still felt uncomfortable around the police station. "It makes me feel like a victim. Powerless."

Zane's eyes flew to hers. He knew she was speaking the truth now, having gone slightly off script.

"You might always feel that way," he said softly. "It might never be a place you're totally comfortable with."

She shrugged. "I have to admit, it's easier when you're there."

He walked over and wrapped his arms around her. "But I know you can handle it either way."

She needed to get them off her personal feelings and back on script.

"I know what I want to do!" This was it. The part of the plan Zane and Jon thought whoever was after them would go for. All Caroline had to do was sell it to whoever was listening.

Zane chuckled. "Wow, haven't seen you this excited for a while. What do you want to do?"

"There's that new shop, Taste Unlimited, downtown. It sells all sorts of foods made for picnics, but also wines and desserts."

"Sounds great to me."

"Let's go there and I'll pick out the food and you pick out the wine and dessert. It'll be a crazy hodgepodge and perfect for a picnic. We can even have the picnic in the station if you want to, since I'm sure going to the beach or a park is off-limits for a while."

"I just want to keep you safe."

His statement was part of the script, but she also knew it was true.

"But I guess a little shopping before locking us away at the station isn't a problem. And it sounds like we might come up with some crazy combinations."

Caroline reached over and kissed him. "That will make it even better."

Zane looked at his watch as if he was considering the time. "Okay, let's shower and I want you to take a little nap first. We'll leave for your Taste Unlimited place and their vast offerings in, say, three hours? Then we have to go to the station so I can get some work done."

He phrased it as though he wanted to make sure that was okay with her. As though they hadn't carefully discussed how much time to give whoever was listening so he could have a chance to investigate the store, see if it would be a great place to try to grab Caroline or Zane and formulate a plan.

There were already officers at the store waiting. Watching for anyone who might come in looking to scope out the place. Especially aware of what Damien Freihof looked like.

Caroline and Zane had laid the bait. Now it was time to see what they would catch in their trap.

Chapter Fifteen

A little more than three hours later, Zane was pulling into a spot in Taste Unlimited's parking lot. Lillian sat in the passenger seat next to him. Her normal dark hair was covered by a brown wig and she wore a pair of large sunglasses.

Not much could be done about her darker skin— Lillian's heritage was Latina, as opposed to Caroline's light skin and freckles. Lillian wore a long-sleeve shirt and a maxi skirt that covered most of her legs, but that was as much as could be done.

If anybody got a close look at Lillian, they would know she wasn't Caroline. But hopefully it would be enough. And thankfully Caroline currently waited at a safe house a few miles away. A protection detail with her. Knowing she was safe was the only thing that allowed Zane to be able to focus on this mission.

"Ready?" Zane asked Lillian.

"Yep. Let's get this son of a bitch."

Zane smiled. Nobody messed with Lillian who didn't live to regret it.

"So far we haven't seen anything unusual," Jon's voice said inside Zane's ear. He was in a van with a painter's logo, parked just outside the front door of the shop. Inside were detectives Wade Ammons and Raymond Stone, one working the register, the other the sandwich counter. The owners of Taste Unlimited had been fully cooperative, a fact for which Zane was truly grateful.

"Okay, Jon. We're going in."

"Roger that."

Another undercover officer would enter the store after Zane and Lillian and together they'd all be looking for anyone who seemed suspicious or overly interested in either Zane or Lillian's Caroline.

"All right, let's do this," Zane said to Lillian. She also could hear Jon through her earpiece.

Zane jumped out of the truck and hustled around it to open the door in a grand romantic gesture. Knowing the guy might be watching them even right now, Zane immediately tucked Lillian into his shoulder. She did her part, burying her head into his chest, wrapping both her arms around his waist.

To anyone else it would just look like a loving couple on their way to pick up food for a picnic with just a tad too much PDA. He hoped.

Zane glanced around without trying to give the appearance he was doing so. There was only so much he could do without giving himself away. He had to trust the people on the team. They were good at their jobs and had a much more natural vantage point, able to watch without being noticed.

He'd worked with Wade and Raymond for years in the department. Jon was also top at his job. Zane knew he could trust them all.

Once inside the store, he and Lillian split up.

"Pick us out something good," Lillian said to him, playing her part. She was keeping her sunglasses on even though they were inside. It would look unusual, but better than giving someone a clear picture of her face.

They were inside the store for about five minutes when Jon reported.

"Okay, we've got an SUV with tinted windows pulling up on the east side of the parking lot. Near the back exit. Single male, midforties, about to enter through the front door."

"Roger that," Zane murmured as everyone else did the same.

Zane positioned himself in a row where he could see the front entrance while appearing to be studying a label on a bottle of wine. He saw the man enter.

Nothing about the man's actions could be considered casual. He looked down one aisle, then another. He didn't do anything overtly suspicious, but neither did he look like the other customers. If they weren't looking for someone who had nefarious intentions, no one would probably take much notice of the man at all.

But expecting a killer? This man fit the bill.

He glanced over at Zane, then looked away quickly. Zane pretended to study the wine bottle as he watched the man pick up a jar of olives and do the same.

"Lillian, get in position by the back door. Let's see if we can tempt him into making a move." Jon's voice came over everyone's earpiece. "I'm running this guy through facial recognition, but unless we get super lucky, we're not going to get a response in time for it to be helpful."

The man set the olives on the shelf and began walking.

"He's coming your way, Lil," Zane whispered.

"Roger."

Zane moved through the aisle, wanting to be near in case something went down.

"You've got another couple coming in through the front," Jon said seconds before the door opened and the electronic chime gave its short whistle.

Counting the one pair who had already been inside the store, the man and the new couple, they had a total of five potential suspects.

Jon said what Zane was thinking. "Remember, we might not be dealing with a lone suspect. So don't discount these couples."

Zane heard Wade talk to one duo as they selected products. Lillian still had her back to the man to keep her face hidden. The man was slowly working his way up toward her.

"Lil, he's about seven feet behind you," Zane said, wanting to give her as much of an advantage as possible. From where he stood, he could see her nod her head just the slightest bit.

The new couple who came in knew exactly what they wanted. Grabbed a meat and cheese platter and a bottle of wine and were soon paying Wade at the register.

The suspicious man still hadn't made any moves, but neither were his actions normal. He was staring at different items up and down the aisles, as if he had no idea what he wanted.

Or he wasn't in here to buy anything at all. Maybe just like the team, he was scoping things out, checking to see if anything was fishy before he made his move.

Zane eased himself back just as Jon made the same call. "Everybody, the main suspect might be scoping, so don't do anything suspicious or draw attention to yourself. We've got a group of three women coming in the door, early twenties. And another single man, African American, midthirties."

Having more people in the store both helped and hurt. It made Zane and the crew less conspicuous, but it also gave them more people to have to watch. Even the group of women couldn't be ruled out.

"Roger," Raymond whispered into the comm unit before turning to the new customers and offering his assistance. Zane looked at the man he still found most suspicious. He seemed to be easing his way toward Lillian.

"He's about five feet from you now, Lil," he said

softly. "Why don't you go check out that counter near the back door? I'm going to hang out near the front door in case he decides he wants to take me instead."

They were counting on the fact that the man would probably use a concealed sidearm to try to get either Zane or Lillian, or both, to leave with him. But in case he had other plans and decided shooting within the store was acceptable, the team all had their own weapons ready. Not to mention SWAT outside, who could be called in on a moment's notice.

Lillian moved toward the back door and Zane followed, still holding the bottle of wine he'd been studying but with his left hand so he'd be easily able to draw his gun from the holster with his right.

When the guy shifted his weight back and forth on his feet—deciding if this was worth it?—then moved toward Lillian, Zane was sure they had their guy.

"I think he's about to make a move," Zane said into his comm device. "Get ready to lock it down, Jon."

"Roger."

Zane could see Lillian, looking so much like Caroline with the brown wig, tense just slightly, not enough to be noticeable to a bystander but enough for Zane to be sure she was ready.

"Zane," Jon said. "We've got another single male entering the store. Parked where I would if I was the perp. Backed his car in for an easier getaway."

Damn it, Zane didn't want to split his focus between the guy almost on Lillian and the new one. He couldn't talk easily into his comm unit without the first guy hearing him.

"Zane," Wade said when he got a visual on the man entering the store, "This guy was at the store earlier. Came in, bought a sandwich and left. Big guy. Caucasian. Midtwenties."

That changed things. Someone who had scoped out the store earlier and then parked in a way that made an escape easier?

Suddenly they had two equally potential perps.

"I'm sending in another undercover officer, Joanna Cordell," Jon said. "Zane, you stay with Lillian and the first guy, and Joanna will be on the second."

Joanna had been on the force for a long time. She was in her fifties but was a good officer. Not to mention no one would pay much attention to her. She just looked like a friendly motherly type.

Zane turned and took a couple steps back so he couldn't be heard. "Remember, we need them to make a move before we take them down. We can't arrest anyone for being creepy."

"Roger that," Jon said. "She'll be coming through the door in fifteen seconds. Raymond, you work with her on the new guy. Wade, you get ready to go whichever way is needed."

"Roger." Both men's muffled responses came through.

Zane turned his attention back to Lillian and the agitated guy. He was still moving closer to her and seemed to be more nervous. He picked up one more bottle, then put it down, before walking right over to Lillian.

"Excuse me, miss?" Zane's hand was at his weapon before the guy even tapped her on the shoulder. But Zane kept his cool. Asking someone a question wasn't a crime.

"Contact," he murmured into his mic for the team to hear.

"Yes?" Lillian responded, keeping her face slightly averted from the guy. Depending on how familiar he was with how Caroline looked, this would play out for only a minute at best before he realized it wasn't really her.

"Do you know anything about capers?"

Capers?

To Lillian's credit, she kept her wits about her. "You mean, like the stuff that goes in Greek salads?"

The guy looked visibly relieved. "Yes. Exactly. My wife is seven months pregnant and she sent me out demanding capers. And hell if I know what capers are. I thought they might be olives."

This could still be a ploy, but if so, it wasn't a very strategic one. The guy was leading Lillian away from the back entrance, where it would've been so easy to just grab her arm and pull her out, and back toward the middle of the store. Where the damn olives were.

"I'm pretty sure this first guy isn't our perp," Zane said into his comm unit. "I think he's just freaking out because his wife is pregnant and is craving specialty food. But I'll keep watching."

"Joanna is moving in toward guy number two," Wade murmured. "We probably need to get Lillian close to the back entrance again if we're eliminating guy number one as a suspect."

"Let's have someone tail guy one when he leaves, just in case he got spooked." Seeing if the guy really did have a pregnant wife and asking him some general questions about Taste Unlimited wouldn't be hard.

"Roger that," Jon said from out in the van.

Zane turned to the side so no one could tell he was speaking. "Wade, can you move over to help the pregnancy guy out? That will free Lillian to move back toward the exit to see if we get a rise out of suspect two."

Over the comm unit Zane could hear Wade ask Lillian and the pregnancy guy if they needed any help. The guy told Wade about the capers and Lillian eased away, wishing him luck. Wade did his best to figure out what the hell capers were and where they were located.

"The second guy is staring at Lillian," Jon said. Zane couldn't see them from the aisle he was located in. "Be sure to keep your face averted toward the east wall, Lil. He's studying you pretty hard."

"Roger," Lillian said. She moved from the olive section, away from Wade and the pregnancy guy, back to where she'd been perched before, right by the exit. She studied the trail mix and different bags of nuts and seeds there. Carefully picking up one container after another and reading the back.

Zane worked himself closer so he could have visual contact with Lillian and the guy.

He was definitely studying her.

He took a few steps down the aisle toward her, but then the three twentysomething gals came around the corner. They were laughing and joking and asked his opinion about something.

As soon as he had the attention of three attractive women, the man obviously forgot about Lillian altogether. Zane watched discreetly for a few more minutes to make sure this wasn't part of a ploy.

It wasn't. The guy was here because either he liked the sandwich he'd gotten earlier or he figured out a lot of attractive women hung out at Taste Unlimited. Or both.

"You see this, Jon?" Zane asked.

"Yeah. Doesn't look like he's our perp, either. Just out trolling for women. I'll still have someone follow him, just in case."

They stayed at the shop another thirty minutes, watching as a number of people came in and out, but none of them approached either Lillian or Zane. When they'd been there over an hour total, Zane finally decided to call it.

"This is a bust, you guys. Whoever was listening isn't coming. Perp either decided it wasn't worth the risk or somehow spotted us and left."

"I agree," Jon said. "But in case you're still being

watched, you and Lillian buy some stuff and head back out to your vehicle. The bugs might still be useful. We'll try again soon."

It just meant another night where Caroline wasn't safe. Another day where they couldn't get on with their lives. Couldn't be together just as a normal couple.

He wanted to give her that—give them *both* that—so badly he could taste it.

They got a bottle of wine and threw in a few food items, paid Wade at the register and walked out the front door.

"Sorry, Zane," Lillian murmured. "Maybe I didn't look enough like Caroline to draw the perp in."

Zane shrugged. That might be true, but there wasn't anything they could do about that. "Maybe. But if so, it wasn't due to lack of effort on your part."

"Like Jon said, we'll try again. Just because it didn't work this time, doesn't mean it won't work at all."

"Yeah. We've just got to come up with another location that is secure but also—"

Jon's voice interrupted their conversation. "Zane, we've got a problem."

"What?"

"I just received an SOS from the safe house. Caroline's in trouble."

Zane and Lillian both dropped their groceries and sprinted for the truck.

Chapter Sixteen

Caroline didn't like being out of the action, but she understood the need for it. She wasn't a trained law enforcement officer. Yes, she'd done some significant self-defense training since the attack, but that didn't mean she knew enough for undercover work. She was nowhere as good as Zane and Lillian and Jon.

They were capable. More than capable. Skillful. But still it was hard being protected here inside the safe house knowing they were out there facing possible danger.

It had all been very cloak-and-dagger. She and Zane had napped at Caroline's town house—although neither of them had really slept—then gotten up and ready for their date, talking about normal stuff.

Zane had been crisp and collected, helping lead Caroline into conversations that seemed mundane, normal. Helping her forget there was someone trying to kill them listening on the other end of those transmitting devices.

He rescued her every time she started to flounder,

panicked that she might say something wrong. Once when she'd been getting too flustered, he'd backed her up against the refrigerator and kissed her senseless.

That had made her forget her own name, much less that they were on some supersecret mission.

When it was time to leave, having given the bad guys plenty of time to scope out Taste Unlimited and figure out how to make their move, Zane mentioned he needed to go to the bank before their date. He and Caroline had walked into the bank together.

A few minutes later, Zane and Lillian, wearing the same outfit as Caroline, had walked out and gotten into Zane's truck.

Caroline had been escorted out of the bank by a plainclothes officer named Gareth Quinn about fifteen minutes later and taken to a safe house, which was actually just a couple miles from the Taste Unlimited store. He'd explained how he understood why she wouldn't want him staying in the house with her and would stay out in the car.

Captain Harris's—her adoptive uncle Tim's—doing, no doubt. She loved the man and had known him since birth, but he couldn't seem to let her attack go. Did he really think that Caroline was so fragile that she wouldn't even want to be around a male police officer for a couple hours? So the captain had ordered Quinn to wait outside.

That was the problem with family, wasn't it? Even adopted family, like Tim. They loved you, but they never allowed you to change. Caroline was always going to be the victim to them. To her uncle especially, since he worked in law enforcement and saw the worst of humanity. Which sucked, since he was also the captain of police and worked very closely with her bosses.

Zane and Lillian would've been at the shop for almost an hour now. She hoped no news was good news. That not hearing from them meant they had caught whoever was behind all this and were in the process of throwing the book at him. Or them. Whatever.

She knew Zane would call as soon as he had something concrete to tell her. This safe house wouldn't be her home for more than a few hours. She and Zane had considered taking her to his place at the beach but decided the fewer people who knew about that, the better. But she would've rather been there.

A knock on the door froze Caroline's blood. Damn it, would that happen for the rest of her life? Would her mind always automatically go back to the day of the attack whenever she heard a knock? It was one of the things she hadn't been able to get any control over. No matter what, when she heard a knock on the door, her entire body clenched in panic.

She walked to the door, trying to get her fear under control. She was in a safe house with an officer outside. Nobody but law enforcement knew where she was.

But when she opened the door just the slightest bit, a man came crashing through.

Just like what had happened the day she was attacked.

If she thought panic assailed her just at the knock, it was nothing compared to the sheer terror that sucked her under now. Every self-defense move she'd learned, every means of protecting herself, vanished from her mind.

The man pushed her to the ground and Caroline cried out. Scurrying back, getting away from him, was all she could think to do.

She couldn't scurry away fast enough. The man walked over to her and gripped her by her hair. Caroline cried out.

"It's time for you to come with me."

He began pulling and she began to struggle, kicking out toward him, which he just easily sidestepped.

Her terrified mind waited for the blows to come. The blows that would break her bones, deliver pain she hadn't thought was possible, like it had before. Somewhere in the back of her mind she knew this wasn't Paul Trumpold. He'd been younger, stronger. Had delighted in her pain. This man was not as fit, was older. Didn't seem intent on delivering physical blows.

But when she looked up into the doorway, she swore she saw Trumpold. His dark hair and good looks that had fooled everyone, hiding a monster.

Caroline wretched, vomiting up the entire contents of her stomach.

She struggled to remember a self-defense move, to force herself to do more than just squirm and kick at the man. She sobbed in frustration as he pulled her toward the door, grabbing at his hand to relieve the pressure in her scalp.

"If you don't come with me, I'll be forced to kill you here."

The man sounded like he almost regretted that fact, but Caroline knew she couldn't let him take her from the safe house. She knew firsthand the sort of pain the human body could endure before death. She didn't want to die here, but she couldn't let him take her from this house.

But then he was gone, his hold of her scalp ripped free as he went flying past her deeper into the room.

It took her a moment to realize there was a tangle of two bodies. And the other one was Zane.

Lillian stood in the doorway, gun raised. "Are you okay, Caroline?" she asked, her eyes surveying the room rather than looking at her.

"Y-yes. I'm okay."

Zane was fighting with the other man, if you could call it much of a fight. Zane was younger, stronger and obviously enraged.

Lillian stepped in, gun still raised to chest level. She scoped out the rest of the room.

"Did the guy come in alone?" she asked, ignoring the punches being thrown by Zane and the intruder.

"I...I don't know." Caroline barely got the words out. "I thought I saw a second man standing at the door, but I'm not sure." She also thought the man was Paul Trumpold, but he was dead. Caroline knew she couldn't trust her own mind.

Lillian quickly made her way into the one bedroom of the safe house, the bathroom and the kitchen.

"We're clear here," she said into some sort of communication unit.

Jon came running through the door, looked at Caroline huddled up against the wall and Zane and the other man still rolling on the ground throwing punches at each other.

"Zane, enough," Jon said. "We need to question him, not put him in the hospital."

Caroline watched Zane pull himself together and get off the man, who lay moaning on the floor. Both Lillian and Jon had their weapons trained on him. He wasn't going anywhere.

"Cuff him," Zane told Jon, then walked over to Caroline.

She wanted to go to him, to meet him halfway, but couldn't seem to get herself off the wall.

He held his arms out in front of him, the way someone would do if they were proving they meant no harm or sudden movement. She knew then that she must look as frightened and horrified as she felt.

"Zane," she whispered his name and fell into him. He caught her and lowered them both to the ground, his arms wrapped securely around her.

"Are you hurt?" he asked. "Do we need to get you medical attention?"

"No," she whispered. "He didn't hurt me."

For the longest time they said nothing else, just held each other. She could hear Jon read the guy his rights before they cuffed him. Multiple officers came in and out of the safe house, including Gareth Quinn, who evidently had been knocked unconscious in the car on the street but then came to and called in reinforcements.

Zane just sat against the wall holding Caroline the whole time.

"Let's get you home," Zane finally said.

"Don't you need to go question that guy or something?"

"It will wait. They'll get all his info, but they won't start questioning him without me."

Caroline just tucked herself into his arm. She didn't want to look around. Didn't want everyone to know that they'd been right to be so protective of her. That when literal push came to shove, Caroline had frozen.

That she was as weak as everyone thought.

She'd sworn she'd never be a victim again. Had gone through hundreds of hours of therapy and physical training to keep from being a victim again, but when the crisis moment had come, she'd just folded and begun to cry.

Caroline wanted to cry now. Huddled against the door of Zane's truck, staring blankly out the window, she wanted to bawl her eyes out. She'd been fighting so hard for her independence, swearing she could handle herself, that she was so strong.

One knock on a door and two minutes of a man pushing through had shown her otherwise. She was never going to be okay again.

"Caro," Zane whispered, not trying to touch her. "Are you sure you're not hurt? Don't hide it if you are. Tell me."

"No, he didn't hurt me. Didn't hit me at all. Was just pulling me out the door by my hair. You're more hurt than I am." She didn't look away from the window as she said it.

They rode in silence until Zane eventually pulled up to his beach house. They went up the stairs, Zane unlocking the door, then checking to make sure the house was secure. Caroline didn't wait outside for him to finish this time. She entered, then crossed all the way to the living room to the outside deck. She crossed to the railing, staring out at her beloved ocean. From this direction she couldn't see the sun that was beginning to set but knew it was by the purple hues being cast over everything.

"Caro." She heard Zane from the doorway. "Tell me what's wrong. It's more than just the guy breaking in, isn't it?"

She could hear him come a little closer.

"Although, that's upsetting enough for anyone. To think you're safe, that the danger is elsewhere, but it's not. That's scary. And not just to you, to anyone."

He fell into silence when she didn't say anything. How could she make Zane understand? He'd always been so strong, so capable. Never plagued by doubt or frozen into inaction.

Not like her.

It was a crippling thing to realize all the progress you thought you'd made—you'd worked and scraped and clawed for—was just a figment of your imagination.

"He knocked on the door." The words were out of her mouth before she could stop them.

Zane didn't push, just came and stood by her at the railing.

"Trumpold knocked. The day he attacked me, he knocked on my door." Caroline knew this was a sore spot for Zane. That he blamed himself for not being the one who had knocked on her door that day. But he didn't draw the conversation to him or his guilt. She appreciated it. Appreciated the strength in his silence.

"So when this guy knocked, I panicked. I should mention that I always panic when someone knocks on my door. God forbid you be the poor package delivery guy in my neighborhood. He must think I live on the verge of a nervous breakdown." She tried to laugh, but it didn't sound the least bit amused even to her own ears.

"It's an understandable trigger, Caro. You know that, right?" he said softly.

"Oh, God, yes, I understand that. I have spent more time in therapy talking about knocks on doors than anything else. It's ridiculous." She tapped her knuckles against the railing. "Even knowing it's me, watching my own knuckles hit the wood, I still get slightly nauseous at the sound."

Zane nodded, not saying anything. She couldn't blame him. What could you say to that?

"But I thought it was probably that officer, Gareth Quinn. And I knew I was being a complete coward. So I opened the door."

She took a deep breath.

"It was only opened a crack when he pushed his way through, slamming the door open."

"Just like Trumpold," Zane finished for her.

"Yes." Caroline could barely get the syllable out.

Zane put his hand over hers on the railing. "I'm so sorry."

She pulled her hand out from under his. "But that's not it, not really. If that is what had happened and the dude had scared the life out of me and you'd gotten there just in time to save the day, I'd be fine with that."

"I don't understand. I thought he didn't hurt you."

"He didn't, Zane. He was planning on dragging me out of the safe house, told me he was going to kill me, but you got there in time."

"That's good, right?" He obviously couldn't understand the distress tainting her tone.

"I froze."

He didn't ask what she meant. He'd been in law enforcement too long not to understand.

"I've spent so much time studying self-defense since the attack. Months of classes. Hundreds of hours. But when he forced his way in, it was like I forgot it all."

"Caro—"

She shook her head. "I can see it all playing in my head like it's a movie. And I want to scream at that girl on the ground, 'What's the matter with you? You know how to break his hold. Hell, you know how to break both his arms. Do it!'"

Her hands clenched into fists. "I just laid there on the ground, crying, Zane. I even vomited. That guy wasn't as fit as Trumpold, wasn't as strong, hadn't stunned me the way Trumpold had with his first two punches. But I just laid there, blubbering. I don't know what would've happened if you hadn't gotten there when you did."

"Caroline, it happens. People freeze up. Even in law enforcement it happens."

His matter-of-fact tone, devoid of anything that could be considered condescending or pitying, helped her in ways he couldn't possibly know.

"I hate myself. I hate myself for being so weak. A victim." She turned away from the view of the ocean and leaned her back against the railing. "Again."

Zane came to stand right in front of her, his hands on her shoulders. "There's nothing about you that's weak, Caro. And you're no victim. You were stunned. A situation you couldn't possibly have expected caught you off guard. It happens."

She didn't want to look at him, but he caught her chin with his thumb and finger and forced her to look up. Forced her to look into those rich brown eyes, where she didn't see anything close to pity or concern. Didn't even see love.

She saw respect, and it meant more to her than all the other emotions could've meant combined.

"We got there when we did, and thank goodness," Zane continued. "Because those punches I got in on that guy, I needed them, and they're probably the only ones I'll legally get."

She couldn't help but smile a little at that.

"But I have no doubt you would've bounced back, Caro. That training you've done, it would've filtered its way back into your mind, into your muscles. You wouldn't have let yourself be taken by that guy. I would bet every cent I have in this life and the next one that you would've taken him down in the next few minutes."

Caroline leaned into his chest. "I just wish I had a replay button. That I could go back and do it again. Make it different."

He wrapped his arms around her like he planned to never let her go. "Believe me, I've wished for one of those too. But we can only move forward. All I know is that you have the inner strength to withstand damn near anything."

Chapter Seventeen

Zane didn't go back into the station that night. Caroline and her needs were more important to him than questioning the perp they'd caught right away. Plus, Zane probably needed a little more cooling-down time anyway.

He'd probably lose his newly reinstated status pretty quickly if he started punching on a suspect in custody.

He had let Jon and Captain Harris know he wasn't coming in until this morning and both had agreed it was the best thing to do. The suspect—Jon informed Zane that the guy's name was Donald Brodey, a name that sounded vaguely familiar to him—would wait.

But now Zane was ready. Wanted some answers. Lillian was hanging out with Caroline so Zane could be at the station getting them. He didn't want to take any chances until they knew exactly what was going on. After what happened yesterday, Caroline wasn't as resistant to having Lillian around, which broke his heart.

Caroline's reaction to the break-in at the safe house wasn't unheard of and certainly wasn't anything that should cause her shame. He'd gotten through to her the best he could about that, but he knew she regretted how she'd reacted. But any law enforcement officer knew full well that practicing, drills, sparring were all well and good, but that in the heat of the moment, training didn't always translate to perfect real-world responses.

He wished Caroline could have another chance to fight down the guy breaking through the door, but he damn well hoped it would never happen again. Zane would help her find other ways of making sure she didn't freeze up again that didn't involve her being in actual danger.

Zane found Jon back at the little corner desk beside the copying machine, where the department had so rudely put him when he'd come here initially working the serial rapist case. Nobody in the Corpus Christi PD had wanted an outsider coming in to help with the case. They'd thought Jon would be a hotshot know-it-all.

He'd been neither.

"You know we'll get you a regular desk, Jon. You don't have to be all Harry-Potter-living-under-the-stairs anymore."

Jon smiled. "This desk holds some pretty fond memories for me. Led me to my soon-to-be wife, you know."

Zane smiled too. Couldn't argue with that. Sometimes bad circumstances were what ended up pointing you in the right direction.

"So does the name Donald Brodey seem familiar to you?" Jon got up and handed a file to Zane.

"Vaguely."

"That's because you arrested him eight years ago. Felony breaking and entering coupled with burglary."

Zane opened the file. "Yes. Now I remember. It was one of my first cases as a detective." He studied the mug shot of Brodey from nearly eight years ago. He'd been in his late thirties then, which put him in his midforties now.

"Looks like a pretty cut-and-dried case. His prints were at the scene. He'd already done a couple of years for misdemeanor B and E charges."

Zane's eyes narrowed. "But he always said he didn't commit this particular crime. I remember that."

"Did you believe him?" Jon asked.

Zane shrugged. "Not really. But I have to admit, I might have been more interested in proving my worth to the department than I was interested in listening to some repeat offender argue about his innocence."

"Looks like he served six years. He's been out for about a year and a half."

"Honestly, I haven't thought about Brodey since he went to prison. I definitely wouldn't have pegged him for trying to kill me. For a damned B and E conviction." Zane closed the file.

"Well, he wanted to talk to you."

"Then let's give the man what he wants."

They cleared it with the captain and had Brodey brought to an interview room from holding. The man was definitely bruised from their tussle yesterday, but then again, so was Zane.

"Detective Wales." Brodey smirked as Zane and Jon entered.

"Brodey." Zane took the seat directly across from him. Jon took the one at the corner of the metal table. Jon read the man his rights.

"Not going to call for your lawyer, Brodey?"

The older man sat back in his chair. "Nope. Ain't got nothing to say that a lawyer will change."

"I suppose you're innocent of this just like you were innocent all those years ago?"

Brodey's eyes narrowed. "I was innocent of that B and E and you know it."

Zane shook his head. "Is that why you've been sending me all those texts? My 'secret' that would come to light."

"Yeah. You can't hide your secrets forever, Wales." He crossed his arms over his chest.

"And Caroline Gill? What does she have to do with my secrets?"

"Everybody knows the best way to get to you is through Caroline Gill. That's why I was trying to take her yesterday. I knew if I could get her, it wouldn't be any problem to get you to surrender."

"And what were you going to do once I surrendered?"

"You were going to pay for them permanently, Wales. For the lies you told. For the years I lost."

Zane glanced over at Jon, who looked as surprised as he did. For someone who'd always claimed his innocence about a crime eight years ago, Brodey had just confessed to a much bigger one.

"What are you doing, Brodey? Why are you telling me this? You know it's just going to get you sent back to prison."

"Maybe it's worth it. Maybe seeing you pay for your sins is worth the risk of going back to prison."

"You've been out of jail for eighteen months. Why did you decide to just come after me now?"

"Somebody made me see the light. A fellow I think you guys know. Name is Freihof. Damien Freihof."

Brodey had their attention now.

"Freihof put you up to this? To trying to kill both me and Caroline?"

Brodey smiled. "Yep. Helped me to understand that you needed to pay for what you'd done. That I lost years of my life thanks to you."

"But what about Caroline? She never did anything to you, Donald. Why take out some sort of misguided revenge on her?"

Brodey looked down for just a minute and shifted in his chair. Then he looked back up at Zane. "Did you know I had three kids when you put me in jail, Wales? They needed their daddy and they lost him. Because of you. Sometimes innocent people get hurt. Your girlfriend was like my children."

"How did you know where Caroline would be yesterday?"

"I planted bugs in her house so I could listen to what you said."

"We found those. But we never said anything about where Caroline would be staying." Zane knew full well they wouldn't have given that information away in their conversation, knowing someone was listening.

"Yeah, but you didn't find the device I put in your truck. I could hear all your conversations there too. I knew you were using that other lady as bait to try to draw me out."

Zane grimaced. They hadn't even thought about a transmitting device in their vehicles. But they should have.

"So I followed you to the bank yesterday," Brodey continued. "Then followed her from there instead of you."

It was a smart plan and had almost worked. If Brodey had moved a little quicker. If he'd knocked Gareth Quinn a little harder on the head so the other man didn't wake up so quickly and report the problem, Brodey would've gotten away with it.

Zane and Jon spent the next few hours questioning Brodey, trying to get as much information as they could about Damien Freihof. Brodey wouldn't admit to anything that happened in Big Bend but gave fairly consistent answers to questions about yesterday's attack.

Two days ago he'd broken into Caroline's town house and planted the transmitting devices. He'd then immediately gone over to Zane's house and trashed it. They'd missed catching him by only thirty minutes.

Brodey knew his best bet was to get Caroline alone. To kidnap her and draw Zane out. Realizing the info Zane and Caroline were providing in her town house was a trap, Brodey decided to use their own plan against them.

And Damien Freihof was at the heart of it all. Encouraging Brodey. They'd never met, but Freihof had spent the last two weeks by phone and video messaging convincing Brodey of the justice of taking Zane down. Brodey had agreed.

By midafternoon, Zane had done all the questioning he could. Brodey had written down his confession. His intent. Brodey would be going back to jail, probably for the rest of his life.

Zane and Jon filed the paperwork they needed, then went to Zane's house to break the good news to Caroline and Lillian.

It wasn't often in a law enforcement officer's career where the bad just up and admitted to a crime, even signing a confession. Sure as hell made the case easier.

They explained everything while Caroline cooked a simple spaghetti dinner with salad.

"So it looks like Brodey will be going away for a long time," Zane finished.

"Omega Sector still has to catch Freihof, but Brodey's failure to kill you at least slows his plans considerably. It will take a lot of time and effort to convince someone else to take on the job of trying to kill you," Jon said.

"Is that what you think this Freihof guy will do? Just keep trying to find people to convince to hurt us?" Caroline asked.

Jon shook his head. "Honestly, no. I think this is a game for Freihof, with rules. Rules that he establishes, but rules nonetheless. I think for each target he has one puppet—for lack of a better word—that he's created and molded."

"With Fitzy, that was Curtis Harper," Lillian said.

Jon nodded. "Exactly. Freihof convinced Harper to kill SWAT member Ashton Fitzgerald. When that didn't work, I think that part of the game was over. Freihof doesn't seem to be going after the same people more than once."

Zane looked over at Caroline, loving the relief that was evident on her face. He reached over and grabbed her hand.

"Until we arrest Freihof, none of us are completely safe, but probably the part of the game involving the two of you is over for him."

"Thank goodness," Caroline murmured under her breath. "I mean, I know that's probably wrong of me to say, since if he's finished with us, it means he's just moving on to someone else."

"Nothing wrong with being thankful that you're out of a madman's scope," Lillian said around a bite of pasta. "And we're going to do our damnedest to make sure Freihof doesn't have the time or means to target someone else."

Caroline smiled. The first real smile he'd seen from her since they were hiking in Big Bend, before all of this started. Zane squeezed her hand. "I'm going to have to take you out so you can finish your Big Bend hike."

"Maybe in a few months. I'm itching to get back to work right now. Back to some sort of normal."

Zane didn't blame her. Caroline needed the parts of her life she had control over. Her job as a paramedic was a big aspect of that. "I'm sure the hospital won't mind having you back a couple days early from vacation."

"Speaking of, I've got to go back to all that wedding nonsense at Omega. It's out of control." Lillian sighed dramatically.

Jon smiled. "Excuse you, I happen to be a big part of that 'wedding nonsense.'"

"I know. You're almost as bad as Sherry."

"Be sure to tell Sherry I can't wait to see her," Caroline said. "Just a few more days."

"I will. It will be nice to have a drama-free weekend for a change."

Chapter Eighteen

The first sight of a broken ankle at a bike accident the next day had Caroline feeling great. That probably made her a little weird, but she didn't care. She was back at work, at a job she knew she was good at. She hated that the cyclist was in so much pain but loved having something to physically do with her hands. With her brain.

How she'd reacted when Donald Brodey broke into the safe house two days ago still stung. But Zane was right: she couldn't let that paralyze her. Couldn't let that stop her forward progress or growth. He'd talked about helping her with some situational awareness exercises and training where she could be caught off guard.

She smiled as she helped brace the young man's foot in preparation to move him into the ambulance. Zane helping her improve these skills would make her more ready for anything that came her way. Any training that made her less of a victim, she was up for.

But more important, it meant that Zane wasn't planning on running back to his little pocket of Corpus Christi after this was all over, never to be seen again. She didn't know if he was going to continue to work for the police department—although everyone had to admit, he'd flowed right back in as if he'd never left—but he wasn't going to disappear again.

She wasn't exactly sure where that left them personally. Eventually they'd need to broach the subject. But right now, sleeping in his arms every night in the house he'd bought for them, the house he hadn't been able to force himself to sell or even rent to someone else? It was enough for her.

They drove the cyclist back to the hospital and Caroline and Kimmie made a beeline for the coffee shop. They'd already been going for four hours in a twelve-hour shift, and you never knew when an emergency call would come in. So you took advantage of coffee breaks while you could.

"I don't think you've stopped smiling all day," Kimmie said as they paid for their brew, preferring the specialized coffee at the shop over the muck that often waited in the free areas of the hospital.

"I'm sorry. I'll start frowning immediately."

Kimmie smacked her lightly on the arm. "You know I think it's great. Although I'm sure that guy with the broken ankle thought you were some sort of sadist—so happy about his pain."

Caroline chuckled. "Yeah, that probably wasn't sensitive."

"I'm assuming your happiness has to do with the arrest of the guy who was trying to kill you."

Caroline added sugar to her coffee. "It's definitely a relief."

Kimmie nudged her. "And don't think it escaped my notice that Zane Wales dropped you off at work this morning."

Caroline tried not to blush. "It was on his way, since he's working at the police station."

"And because you guys were making wild, passionate monkey love all last night, weren't you? Gosh, he is so gorgeous, Caroline. Sigh. I want a super hunk like that."

Out of the blue, Caroline pulled Kimmie in for a hug.

Kimmie hugged her back—as Caroline had no doubt she would—and laughed as they broke apart. "What was that for? We've been partners for nearly eighteen months and I don't think we've ever hugged."

Caroline had resented being partnered with Kimmie. She'd known Uncle Tim had done it because he'd deemed that, after the attack, Caroline needed to work with a woman. Someone nonthreatening and lighthearted. Caroline had tried to never let her resentment show to Kimmie; after all, it wasn't Kimmie's fault she was the most perky, sweet partner they could find. Tim had done what he'd thought was best for Caroline.

Ended up he'd been right. Kimmie was probably the best partner Caroline could've had for the past year and a half. Not because she wasn't a man, but because she was hardworking, enthusiastic, and wanted to learn what Caroline had been ready to teach.

Caroline smiled. And Kimmie was always perky.

"You're a great partner, Kimmie. And a good friend. I just wanted to hug you."

Kimmie hugged her again quickly. "I just wanted to get another one in before you go back to non-hugging mode." She pulled away and they walked down the hallway with their coffee.

They'd barely finished half their cups before they got the call. A warehouse fire down near the oil district. Multiple injuries, utter chaos. An all-hands call.

Caroline and Kimmie dumped their coffee and ran for the ambulance, pulling out of the hospital parking lot rapidly along with other ambulances. Fire and rescue vehicles would be joining them on-site.

As they pulled up to the location, Caroline could see it was worse than she'd thought.

She turned to Kimmie. "The fire chief will be calling out orders. It will be pretty chaotic, so just take it one patient at a time. Don't get overwhelmed."

Caroline had worked only one other fire like this, about five years ago. She'd gotten a little panicked and didn't want the same thing to happen to Kimmie.

They jumped out of the ambulance and reported over to the fire chief, who was barking out orders. He pointed at Caroline and Kimmie.

"Office workers. Southeast corner." He pointed in the general direction. "Smoke inhalation mostly. Evaluate, get the most severely injured to the main hospital. Gill, coordinate and see who needs to go to the local medical center if the main hospital ER can't take them."

It was a big job, to coordinate what patients would go where, but Caroline appreciated the trust the fire chief was putting in her. She was one of the most seasoned paramedics out here. She wouldn't let him down.

"Let's go, people." The EMTs and paramedics—EMTs with more schooling—all followed after Caroline. She split them up into groups and soon everyone had a job to do caring for the injured.

Caroline spent the next six hours coordinating between hospitals and the EMTs, evaluating burn and smoke inhalation victims and getting them where they needed to be. This fire couldn't have happened at a worse spot for casualties. A factory with hundreds of people inside had been affected.

Things were just starting to slow down enough for Caroline to eat a protein bar, something every paramedic kept stashed for situations just like this where a meal wasn't possible. She washed it down with another bottle of water, although she'd been careful to keep herself hydrated throughout the day. She didn't want to end up as someone needing medical attention rather than giving it.

When she had a short break, she grabbed her phone to text Zane.

Massive fire in oil section. Won't be done for a while.

His response was almost immediate.

Be safe. Text me when you're done.

She looked over at the firefighters. They seemed to be getting it under control. Most of the critical victims had been seen and escorted to hospitals and medical centers in the greater Corpus Christi area.

Caroline scoped out the scene. They'd done a good job here today. Loss of life had been minimal thanks to the work of the firefighters and EMTs.

"Hey, Caroline, somebody was looking for you. An EMT," Kimmie said. Caroline had been split up from her partner for most of the day. She pointed to the far side of the building. "Around the corner there. Someone else told me, so I don't know what it's about. Sorry. Want me to go ask?"

Caroline grabbed a protein bar. "No, you stay here and eat this. Take five minutes. You've been working hard today. We all have. I'll go see what's needed."

Kimmie smiled. "Thanks. Wanna hug?"

Caroline rolled her eyes, knowing the woman was kidding. "Yeah. It can be our new thing."

She jogged over to the far side of the building. It was much quieter over there, away from the action. An EMT was crouched down near the back corner.

"Hey, is everything okay?" Caroline asked. "I heard you needed me."

The woman glanced over her shoulder at Caroline.

"Yeah, do you mind coming over here? I think you should see this."

Caroline prayed it wasn't a body, although she didn't see how it could be in such a small space.

She squatted next to the woman and looked into the hole where she stared. Caroline didn't see anything but dirt.

"What are we looking at?" she asked.

Caroline felt a prick at the back of her neck and swatted at whatever bug had bitten her. A few seconds later the woman stood. Caroline tried to stand too, but found herself dizzy.

"Whoa. I think I need to eat something besides a protein bar." She looked back at the hole again. "I'm sorry. What did you want me to see here?"

The woman didn't answer and Caroline turned to look at her again.

She was spinning.

The entire world was spinning.

This wasn't low blood sugar from not eating enough. She'd been drugged.

Caroline looked at the woman again and realized she wasn't really wearing an EMT uniform, just similar colors.

"Who are you?" Getting the words out were more difficult than they should be.

"I'm the person who's going to show the world what a liar you are, Caroline Gill. Finally show everyone what you've done and how my brother's death was your fault."

Caroline tried to stand again but couldn't. She began to crawl away, but much more slowly than she wanted. Her muscles refused to work. She held on to consciousness for as long as she could, even knowing she was fighting a losing battle against whatever drug the woman had given her.

"My brother was a doctor, so I know a little about temporary paralytic drugs," the woman said, inching her face closer to Caroline. "You should never have lied about him, Ms. Gill."

Through the fuzziness in her mind Caroline realized who the woman was. She was the sister of Paul Trumpold, the man who viciously attacked and raped Caroline.

And she thought Caroline had made up the whole story.

She clawed through the dark to try to keep hold of consciousness, knowing this woman intended to harm her, but couldn't do it. Her panic got even worse as she saw someone who looked just like Paul Trumpold standing behind her. As Caroline laid her face on the ground, the woman did the same, facing her.

"Don't worry. We'll talk soon."

The vicious hatred in the woman's eyes was the last thing Caroline saw before the darkness overtook her.

Chapter Nineteen

Zane sat back in the chair at his desk in the Corpus Christi Police Department. When he'd come back in this morning, instead of having to work in the conference room, since he had no desk assigned to him, he'd found his old desk back in place. His old chair at it and nameplate on the front.

Almost like he'd never left.

He would've thought there would've been some hard feelings, either about him returning or about him leaving in the first place. And maybe there was. But as a whole the department had banded together and welcomed him back into their midst.

Zane had to admit leaving again would be difficult. He missed detective work. Even now that they had found the person trying to hurt him and Caroline, he didn't know if he could walk away. The people he worked with here were family. They understood what the attack on Caroline had cost him and supported him—then and now—the best way they could.

Today that had been dragging his desk and chair back to where they'd once been.

But the part of him that enjoyed sitting in this chair, the part of him that had missed law enforcement work every day for the past eighteen months since he'd quit, knew that something wasn't right.

Donald Brodey's arrest. His confession. All of it. As much as Zane wanted it to be perfect and tidy, it wasn't. It just didn't sit well with him.

Something wasn't right.

Jon walked over and leaned on the corner of the desk. "Looks like they're carving out a permanent place for you here."

Zane leaned back, stretching his legs out in front of him. "Nice of them, I have to admit."

"You going to stay?"

"I think so. It's not like I have any other job around right now. They're still picking up pieces of my Cessna in Big Bend."

"Not to mention you miss police work." Jon's eyebrow rose, daring him to deny it.

Zane shrugged. "It's true. I do."

"You're good at it, Zane. Got a natural talent and a good temperament for it."

"I know."

"Plus, that incredible humbleness."

Zane chuckled, but then it faded out. "The only problem is, right now my detective spider senses are telling me there's something wrong with Donald Brodey."

Jon sat at the chair by Zane's desk. "What about him?"

Zane shrugged. He wasn't exactly sure what he meant and didn't want to bog Jon down if his fears amounted to nothing. "I know you need to go. I don't want Sherry getting mad at me because I kept the groom away for too long."

"I've got an hour before I need to leave for my plane. Plus, Sherry is capable of handling anything thrown her way. One of the things I love most about her."

Jon and Sherry were a good fit. Partners in every sense of the word.

"Do you have any wild parties coming up? In your last few days of singlehood?"

Jon shook his head. "Nah. The guys and I will probably go out for a few beers, but I'm not interested in a strip club or the 'normal' bachelor stuff."

Zane wasn't actually surprised. "Oh yeah?"

"Once you have the one you really want, all of that seems ridiculous, you know? I have no interest in seeing any other naked or partially naked woman besides Sherry."

Zane knew what he meant. He wouldn't go to a strip club now if someone dragged him. It wasn't what he wanted.

Caroline was what he wanted. Today. Tomorrow. The rest of their lives.

Jon leaned back in his chair. "So tell me what you think is going on with Brodey."

"I reviewed his case again this morning. From the original B and E."

"And?"

Zane shifted slightly. "Now, with nearly a decade more experience, I'm looking at the arrest in a different light. Brodey claimed his innocence the whole time. Said someone planted his fingerprints at the scene."

"Do you believe him?"

"I believe we caught another burglar six months later and the evidence suggested he'd been placing fingerprints that weren't his around crime scenes to make himself less of a suspect. I think it's possible that Brodey was telling the truth. That someone did put his prints on the scene."

"Brodey had already been convicted two other times, you know. So it's not like this was some innocent guy off the street who got thrown in jail."

"Actually, that's what convinced me. I went back through his other case files, cases I wasn't part of at all, to see if he claimed his innocence then. To see if that was just his MO."

"And?"

"Nope. Served his time, never claimed innocence once."

Jon shifted in his chair. "Okay. Then, that just supports his claim that he was out for revenge. That's why he came after Caroline—to get back at you."

Zane picked up a pencil on his desk and began twirling it between his fingers. "That's what I thought too. That this Damien Freihof guy had just gotten his claws into Brodey and twisted his thinking. And I have to admit, that's possible."

"But something has you questioning it."

"Brodey wasn't ever violent, Jon. All of his crimes involved breaking into houses where no one was home. The man has a family. Kids."

"You're thinking that it's a pretty big jump to go from a family man with no history of violent crime to kidnapping and attempted murder."

"Yes. Exactly. And moreover, I can see why he would still be mad at me. But Caroline? It would take a pretty hardened criminal to kill her for something I did."

"People change. Jail hardens them. Then someone like Freihof comes along and pushes them in a certain direction, even one they wouldn't normally take on their own."

"Yeah, I guess you're right."

Wade Ammons walked through the door of the detective section.

"Hey, Wales, you look pretty good sitting in your old spot. Does that mean you're going to be staying?"

"I'm thinking about it. If you guys and the captain really want me back around."

The younger man smiled. "We do, believe me. It's been hard trying to make this place look good all by myself."

Jon stood. "I've got to move if I'm going to catch my plane. Call me if you need to talk some things through. I'll also keep searching with Omega resources. Make sure we're not missing something."

Zane shook Jon's hand. "Thank you, for everything. I guess Caroline and I will be up this weekend to see you get hitched."

"See you then."

Jon headed out and Zane sat back down at his desk. "Where is everybody, Wade?"

The detectives' desks were on the second floor of the building that housed the police department. It was generally more quiet here than all the uniformed officers' desks and general processing. But it was never this quiet.

"Huge fire down in the oil district started an hour ago. Most of the station is down helping."

"Casualties?"

"Yeah, a lot. A bunch of office workers got trapped. Caroline's down there. Last report was that she was directing ambulance traffic to different hospitals."

It was a crazier day than she'd expected to go back to, but Zane knew she could handle it. She was probably glad to have such a busy day. Caroline liked to keep focused. She excelled at it.

"Let me know if you need any help with anything or if I'm needed at the oil district."

"Will do. Sounds like the worst of it has passed, though."

"I'm going to get Brodey out of holding and talk

to him one more time. I feel like we're missing something."

Wade nodded. "We're gathering everything we know about the last eighteen months of Brodey's life since he made parole. As soon as the file is ready, I'll get it to you."

Interviewing Brodey again wasn't hard, since he was still being housed in the temporary cells inside the department until his bail hearing date. But the man was much less cooperative this time. Sullen almost.

"You still have a right to an attorney, Brodey. You know that," Zane finally said when Brodey hadn't given him nearly as open answers as yesterday. "Do you want a lawyer?"

The man had already signed a confession, so it wouldn't help much. But it was still his right.

"Naw. I don't want no lawyer."

"Tell me more about Damien Freihof. How did he contact you?"

Brodey looked down at his hands. "Freihof called me on the phone. Said he'd been over my case. That he thought you were a crooked cop and that I should take my revenge on you."

"I see."

"I lost a lot of years of my life because of you."

"You already had two strikes before you even came across my radar. So it's difficult to believe that you think I'm responsible for all your woes."

Brodey just crossed his arms and leaned back in his chair, staring at the table.

Zane decided he needed to take another tack. "But okay. What if I said, looking back at the case now, I can see why you said you were innocent. That I agree with you that someone should've looked more closely into your case when we discovered someone was, in fact, planting prints of other criminals."

Brodey straightened for just a moment, looking Zane in the eye. "That's what I told you from the beginning."

"And I was wrong, Brodey, I should've listened. But I was young. Yours was one of my first solo detective cases. I wanted to make a splashy arrest maybe more than I wanted to make sure justice was served."

"You tell my wife that, okay, Wales?" It was the first time Brodey hadn't seemed dour. Seemed legitimately invested in what he was saying. "You tell her that I wasn't lying about not being the one who broke into that house."

"You're going away for attempted murder, Brodey. Why the hell will your wife care about a B and E from eight years ago?"

Brodey seemed to wilt right in front of him. "You're right, I guess. But if it ever comes up, you tell her that, okay?"

Zane tried to get more details from Brodey after that. About Freihof, about Big Bend. But the man wasn't talking.

"I signed a confession. I don't have anything more to say." And that was it. The longer Zane talked, the more silent the older man became.

Zane got a text from Caroline telling him she would be running late and texted her back. He spent some more time with Brodey trying to get him to spill any more details, but the man obviously was done talking.

Finally, Zane had him sent back to his cell. He left the interview room with no more information than when he'd started, besides an odd statement about letting Brodey's wife know he was innocent of a crime that in the greater scheme of things didn't really matter.

As promised, Wade had left a file on Zane's desk about Brodey's whereabouts and activities since he'd been released from prison. He'd been out for eighteen months, unemployed. He and his wife were separated, but not divorced. She'd stayed with him even when he'd been incarcerated. They had three teenage children.

Their financial situation was pretty grim, Zane had to admit. The wife and kids were living in a two-bedroom apartment, and they had missed multiple rent payments. Zane didn't doubt they'd be evicted soon.

There was only one picture of the family. The youngest, Brodey's son, seemed to be using some sort of braces in order to walk. Zane grimaced. Medical bills for an illness or disability could cause even further financial hardship.

He turned the page and everything made more sense for him.

Two months ago, Donald Brodey had been diagnosed with cancer and had less than six months left to live.

No wonder Brodey had wanted him to pass along the message to his wife. The way things were going, with his confession, he would probably never see her again. At least would never see her as a free man.

Maybe Jon was right; maybe finding out he was dying had changed Brodey. Instead of wanting to right any wrongs before he died, he wanted to exact his revenge on Zane. Freihof just happened to contact him at the right time.

Zane leaned back in his chair, the one in which he'd done his best detective work over the years. There was a big piece of the puzzle he still wasn't seeing. He knew that with every fiber of his being.

He just hoped he'd figure it out before disaster struck.

Chapter Twenty

Caroline woke up slowly, feeling like she'd had way too much to drink the night before. But she couldn't remember any drinking.

And why was she sitting if she was waking up the morning after with a huge hangover? Shouldn't she be lying in bed?

She finally pried her eyes open, then immediately closed them again when dizziness and nausea assailed her. She couldn't help the groan that fell from her lips. She tried to raise her hand to her head to help relieve some of the pressure but found she couldn't move her arms.

Then it all came back to her. Not drinking. Drugged. By the sister of the man who had tried to destroy her life.

"Yeah, that chloral hydrate is a bitch, isn't it?" Caroline couldn't tell exactly where the woman's voice was coming from. She was evidently walking around the chair Caroline was bound to. Not helping the dizziness. "Quick to knock someone out, but a little more difficult to recover from."

Caroline felt a sting in her scalp as the woman grabbed her hair and yanked her head back. "But that queasiness? Trust me, that's the best you're going to feel all day. It's just going to get worse from here."

"Who are you?" Caroline pushed the words past the dryness of her throat, her voice sounding strange even to her own ears.

"That's right, we haven't formally met, have we? I'm Lisette Trumpold."

"Paul Trumpold's sister."

The woman snatched Caroline's head back by the hair again. "Don't even say his name." The woman's voice was rising in both pitch and volume. She slung Caroline's head forward. "You ruined his life with your lies. You don't deserve to say his name."

Now it was more than just the drugs that made Caroline want to vomit. After living through the vicious attack by Paul Trumpold, to hear someone defend him—even a family member—made her want to hurl her guts out.

"I never lied about your brother and what that sick bastard did."

The world spun wildly out of control as the back of Lisette's hand connected with her cheek. If she hadn't been tied to the chair, she would've flown out of it.

"Liar!" Lisette screamed right in Caroline's face,

spittle flying everywhere. "I've seen the truth, the real medical reports, not the ones you and your boy-friend fabricated and gave to the police."

Caroline tasted blood in her mouth from where her teeth had scraped the inside of her cheek. She tried to gather her thoughts, figure out exactly what this crazy woman was talking about.

Caroline breathed deeply, trying to take in as many details as possible. Lisette hadn't killed her outright at the fire scene, so evidently she wanted Caroline alive for some reason. That was good. Gave her time to figure out some way of escape.

And she was talking about different medical reports? Caroline had no idea what the hell that meant. Her medical records had definitely been a part of the case against Paul Trumpold, but there had been only one set.

She needed to figure out exactly what Lisette wanted. Then she could better formulate a plan.

"Recognize where we are yet?" Lisette asked.

Caroline forced herself to open her eyes despite the dizziness and nausea it caused. She breathed in and out through her nose, lifting her head and look-ing around. She knew immediately where she was.

She was in the house where she'd lived when Trumpold attacked her. On the floor right under the chair that she was tied to right now, he had beaten her into a coma and raped her.

Caroline could feel the onslaught of panic. Look-ing at the door just a few feet in front of her, she could easily envision the day she'd opened it just a crack and he'd forced his way through. Could feel the pain—a thousand times worse than the slap Lisette had just given her—as his fist connected with her jaw, shattering her cheekbone.

She heard herself whimper, struggling through the effects of the drug to know what was now and what was then. She closed her eyes again, trying to hold on to her sanity.

It was Zane's face in her mind, his voice in her subconscious, that got her through.

All I know is that you have the inner strength to withstand damn near anything.

The words he had said to her after Donald Brodey attacked her at the safe house. She held on to them like a lifeline.

Inner strength. Inner strength. Withstand damn near anything.

Caroline opened her eyes, no longer picturing Trumpold pushing his way through the door.

Paul Trumpold was dead. He could never hurt her again.

His psycho sister, on the other hand, was alive and circling Caroline like some sort of predator. Caroline fought hysteria, knowing she had to work the problem in front of her, just like she did every day as a paramedic.

"You brought me to the house where I used to live," Caroline said as evenly as she could, studying Lisette.

"Yes." Lisette actually looked pretty excited that Caroline recognized it. "I rented it from the new owners."

Caroline resisted the urge to point out how sick that was.

"Are you working with Donald Brodey?"

Lisette began pacing back and forth. "To a degree. He had his usefulness."

That didn't make any sense to Caroline, and it ultimately didn't matter, since he wasn't here to help Lisette, so Caroline decided to try a different tack. The most direct one. "What do you want, Lisette?"

"I want you to pay for what you've done. I want you to tell the truth."

That sounded like what Zane had told her Donald Brodey had said. But Brodey wasn't connected to the Trumpolds in any way that they knew of.

"And what truth is that exactly?"

"I want you to admit to the world that you lied about my brother. About what you said he did to you. I know you lied."

She could see the other woman getting worked up just thinking about it. "Lisette, why do you think I lied? What reason would I have to lie about something like that?"

Lisette stopped her pacing and stared at Caroline. "He said you would say that. That you would say you had no reason to lie."

"Who said that? Brodey?"

Lisette didn't even listen to Caroline, just kept on

talking. "But he showed me the reports. He showed me how you and Zane Wales got together and faked the whole thing."

Caroline shook her head. She didn't want to make Lisette angry, because God knew the woman was already unstable enough, but she honestly had no idea what she was talking about.

"Lisette, I think there was some mistake. Maybe you got the wrong medical reports by accident or something. Mine were very clear about what happened to me."

Lisette stormed over to a nearby table and brought a file back, opening it and holding it in front of Caroline's face.

"This is the medical report that went to the police department."

Caroline didn't need to look at it for long to recognize it. That was very definitely her battered face in the picture. Very definitely pictures of bruises and welts covering half her body. She didn't even try to read the trauma that had been done by the rape itself.

"Yes, that's my medical report." Caroline kept her voice as even as she could, swallowing the tremors.

Lisette flew back to the table and picked up another medical report, holding it in front of her again. "But this is the actual medical report after your socalled attack, isn't it?"

Caroline studied the file, unsure at first of what she was looking at. It was definitely her, but with much less trauma.

Then she remembered.

"Lisette, this is also a medical report for me. But it wasn't after my rape. This was from two months before. I was accosted by a man during one of my calls as a paramedic. He was robbing a convenience store and pushed me over trying to flee from police. My medical report was going to be used as part of his prosecution."

Lisette just stood there, smiling.

"What?" Caroline finally asked.

"That's exactly what he said you'd say. He was right about everything. You don't have any remorse at all, do you?"

"Look, those medical reports are two separate incidents."

"Not according to the dates," Lisette spat.

"What?"

"The dates are the same."

"Then it was a mistake. A typo. Or someone deliberately changed them to try to trick you."

"Or you and Zane Wales turned in a completely false medical report in order to get my brother arrested. You weren't nearly as hurt as you pretended to be."

Caroline tried to reason with her. "Lisette, I know you don't want to hear this about your brother. I'm sure you loved him."

Caroline had a brother and loved him. Of course, he would never attack a woman and beat her until she went into a coma. But she had to stay focused on reaching Lisette and making her understand.

"Brodey or someone else is feeding you lies, Lisette. Someone is trying to trick you into believing that Zane and I did something we didn't do. We had no reason to frame your brother."

"Donald Brodey has nothing to do with this!" Lisette screamed.

And suddenly it all became so clear to Caroline. No, not Brodey.

Damien Freihof.

He was the one who had manipulated Lisette like this. Or had taken what the woman so desperately wanted to hear and given her reason to believe it.

"Damien Freihof has been lying to you." Lisette's eyes flew to Caroline's at the mention of his name, confirming Caroline's suspicions. "He's using you."

"Freihof has done nothing but show me the truth. You are the one who has been telling lies. But I'm going to make sure the world knows the truth."

"And how are you going to do that?"

"You're going to admit what really happened while I record it."

Caroline wanted to point out that even if she retracted her entire account of what Paul Trumpold did to her, it wouldn't change anything. Trumpold had attacked Jon Hatton and Sherry Mitchell. Had admitted to raping Caroline and six other women. He had stabbed Jon and Sherry both and been about to kill them when Zane arrived and shot him.

In the overall process, Caroline's version of the story didn't even matter. Paul Trumpold would've gone to jail with or without her medical record or testimony.

Although she'd been glad to give both to help make sure Trumpold went to prison for as long as possible.

But bringing this to Lisette's attention would probably just cause her to kill Caroline.

"I don't think changing my statement alone would do anything to clear your brother's name." Not that Caroline would do it anyway. There was no way in hell she would amend, modify or otherwise revise even one single line of the truth about what happened to her.

She looked Lisette straight in the eye. "And I won't change it anyway. If you hurt me, people will be able to tell I was only doing it under duress."

"We'll see about whether you won't change your lies when I start cutting off Zane Wales's fingers." Lisette laughed as Caroline blanched. Caroline had no doubt she meant it. "That's why I want you to call him and tell him to meet you here."

Caroline shook her head. "You might have wanted to ask me to do that before you told me you were going to cut off his fingers."

Lisette reached into the pocket of Caroline's paramedic jacket. "I sort of thought you might say that. So I guess I'll just text him with your phone."

She spoke as she typed. "I need you to come to

my old house ASAP. Something important to show you. Can't talk now."

Caroline watched as Lisette sent the text, then cringed when the phone buzzed in response a few seconds later.

"What is it?" Caroline asked. Lisette read the text from Zane out loud.

"We won't answer him." Lisette smiled at Caroline. "How about that? It'll make it seem all so intriguing."

A few minutes later Caroline's phone rang. No doubt Zane calling when she didn't respond to his text. Lisette just held it until it went to voice mail. It rang again a few seconds later, and Lisette just threw it on the table.

"A missed text and two calls?" Lisette smiled. "A mysterious request to meet him at the scene of the crime? I think it's fair to say our white-hatted hero is on the way."

Lisette walked over to the table and began taking out an assortment of knives and guns. "I'll just get everything ready for when he arrives. I bet he'll knock on the door just like you said my brother did. But this time he'll get the surprise of his life."

Chapter Twenty-One

When Zane got another text from Caroline a few hours after the first telling him about the fire, it was because he figured she'd finally finished her shift, a twelve-hour one that had turned into closer to fourteen hours. He hadn't minded staying to do some more work. Trying to figure out what was missing with Brodey and glancing at some other cases. Detectives rarely got to work one case at a time.

But when he looked down at his buzzing phone for the text he thought would be a request to come get her, he did a double take.

I need you to come to my old house ASAP. Something important to show you. Can't talk now.

Zane couldn't think of any reason Caroline would set foot into that house again. Especially without at least talking to him about it first. He texted back.

What is it?

No response. He waited a few minutes in case she was busy with something, but when she didn't answer at all, he called.

Straight to voice mail.

Called again. Same thing.

Zane didn't panic. It had been a long day for both of them. The fire in the oil district wasn't terribly far from the beach section. Maybe she hadn't wanted to come all the way out here to the station just to drive all the way back to the house for whatever she wanted him to see. He began walking to his truck.

Caroline didn't have her truck, so she couldn't have driven herself over there. Someone had to have taken her, so that might explain why she wasn't answering her phone—she was talking to someone else.

But his gut told him that Caroline wouldn't enter that house again casually. Wouldn't just drive by and go inside for no reason. She was strong enough to handle a visit there, but she wouldn't go without planning.

Zane picked up his pace. Something wasn't right here.

"Wade," he called to the other man as he passed him. He gave him Caroline's previous address. "I need you to look up that address and see who owns it now. Any info. It's where Caroline lived when she was attacked."

"Got it."

"I need it fast, Wade. She just texted me from there."

"She in trouble?"

"Nothing to indicate it. But she wouldn't just go back there without a reason."

"I'll call you with the info."

Zane ran out of the station and to his car. The more time that passed without hearing from Caroline, the more worried he became. She should've at least seen he'd called or texted and responded by now. Given all that was going on, the danger they'd faced, she wouldn't just leave him without any communication.

He was just pulling out of the parking garage when his phone rang. He switched his phone to the hands-free speaker so he could continue to drive without looking at the number.

"Caroline?"

"No, man, it's Jon. Were you expecting a call from her?"

Zane explained what was going on and where he was headed.

Jon cursed under his breath. "I put in a request for Donald Brodey's financial records before I got on the plane. I just got to the Omega office and the report was ready."

This couldn't be good, not if Jon was calling so fast. "What?"

"Last week Brodey had a sizable deposit put into his bank account."

"How sizable?"

"Half a million dollars."

Zane whistled through his teeth. For a man who

was about to go back to prison, that would help his family out quite a bit.

"Well, I discovered Brodey is terminally ill. Only a couple months left to live. So Freihof must have paid him to come after Caroline and me. Which makes more sense to me than him wanting revenge enough to want to kill us."

"That's just it, Zane. I tracked down the money. It didn't come from Freihof."

"Are you sure? I can't imagine he'd just use his real name on an account."

"Someone did use their real name, but it wasn't Freihof who paid Brodey."

"Who was it?"

"A Lisette Trumpold. Younger sister to Paul Trumpold."

Zane stomped on the gas, no longer caring about breaking any speed limits. "Damn it, Jon. Caroline texted me from the house where Trumpold attacked her."

"I think Lisette paid Brodey to take the fall for her handiwork in Big Bend. She knew once we had someone in custody—someone who admitted to the crimes—your guard would be down."

"That's why Brodey didn't really have a lot of details today when I went to talk to him. I thought he was just regretting signing the confession. But really it was because he didn't have details to tell."

"And because he didn't want to lose his payoff,"

Jon finished for him. "I'll call Captain Harris and have him send uniforms to the address."

"Tell him to keep them quiet. If this is a hostage situation, I don't want Lisette to panic. I'm only five minutes out."

Another call beeped in. "I've got to go, Jon."

"Be safe, brother."

The call disconnected and Zane connected to the other one, praying it would be her. "Caroline?"

"No, sorry, man, it's Wade."

"Did you find out anything?"

"The house is owned by a Jack and Marty Smith. They rent it out. Current rental for the month of November is…"

"Lisette Trumpold."

"Yeah, do you know her?"

Zane gritted his teeth, wishing he could make the miles fly by faster. "She's the sister of Paul Trumpold, the man who attacked Caroline."

Wade let out a string of obscenities. Zane couldn't agree more.

"Jon Hatton is calling the captain even as we speak to get squad cars out here. They can't come in blazing, Wade."

"I'll make sure they don't."

"I'm not waiting for backup. I'm going in."

"Be careful."

Zane parked his car two houses down from where he needed to be. If Lisette had Caroline, which at this point he couldn't doubt was the case, he sure as hell wasn't going to just go knocking on the front door. Then Lisette could just kill them both.

Not to mention a knock on that door would scare Caroline. He never planned to knock on any door around her for the rest of their lives.

If Lisette had been sending those texts about Caroline being a liar and Zane keeping secrets, then Freihof had obviously gotten his hooks into her. Convinced her somehow that her brother was innocent and he and Caroline were at fault.

As utterly untrue as that was, it at least made sense.

But Lisette had made a tactical error in bringing Caroline here to this house. Caroline had lived here for years before the attack, and Zane had spent so much time here that it was like he had lived here too. He knew which windows creaked and which deck beams would hold his weight as he climbed up.

Weapon drawn, Zane made his way to the bathroom window on the side of the house. He and Caroline had joked and called that window a pervert's delight. If a Peeping Tom got lucky, he could catch someone in the bathroom, if not, he'd still have a view of almost the entire bottom floor.

He saw Caroline tied to a wooden chair in the middle of the hallway. The pressure in his chest eased. She was alive. That was the most important thing.

And he was damn well going to make sure she stayed that way.

He wasn't sure if Lisette was working alone or

not, and he could bet she was armed to the teeth, so he couldn't just barge in. He prayed the squad cars would follow instructions and not come in lights and sirens blazing.

He slipped up the back outer stairs to the far bedroom. It had a door that led out to the deck and was his best chance of getting into the house unnoticed.

It still wasn't going to be easy.

He put his gun back in its holster as he arrived at the door. He let out a sigh of relief when he realized the new owners hadn't been willing to spring for a new, more fortified one. Applying the right pressure at an angle, he was able to slip his credit card in between the handle and the frame and popped open the door.

Caroline had once locked herself out and had shown him the trick. He'd told her how ridiculous she was not to get that door fixed. If she could get in the door like that, then a burglar could too. She'd laughed, saying it was so much more likely that she would forget her keys than it was for someone to break into her house.

He'd always meant to get that door fixed, even if just to piss her off. Thank God he hadn't had the chance and the new owners hadn't, either.

The door creaked slightly as he opened it and he immediately paused, wincing. But he could hear Caroline downstairs, talking to Lisette pretty loudly. He didn't know if she was doing it to help him, but either way it would cover the noise he was making trying to get to her.

He eased the door closed behind him, not wanting to take a chance on the wind blowing something over if he left it open.

"If your boyfriend doesn't get here soon, maybe I'll just start with your fingers."

"Maybe he's not coming. Maybe he has other things to do with his time besides run over here just because he got a cryptic text from me."

"He'll be here. I have no doubt about it. I've seen the way he looks at you. I saw you kissing in the parking lot of the Silver Eagle last week. That's when I realized what Damien told me had to be the truth."

"Just because Zane and I have a physical relationship?"

"Damien told me that you guys had kept apart for all these months to throw off suspicion about your lies. He told me that once you thought it was safe, you'd get back together. He was so right. Damien was right about everything."

"Damien Freihof is a pathological liar and genius using you to get back at a law enforcement group called Omega Sector. You're his pawn, Lisette. You don't have to be."

Zane grimaced as he heard Lisette strike Caroline. "Don't try to talk to me like you know me. You cost my brother his life. I loved him and you cost him everything."

Zane eased down the hall while Lisette paced back

and forth in a frenzy. Then she went over to a table and pulled out a gun and pointed it right at Caroline's head.

Ice flowed through Zane's veins. He could jump from where he stood at the banister, but Lisette would definitely have time to shoot Caroline before he landed.

Caroline cleared her throat. "All right, Lisette, you want your confession from me? I'll give it to you. Set up the camera."

Zane could finally breathe again when Lisette removed the gun and walked over to set up her camera. Caroline was keeping her head, biding more time. Zane eased down a couple of stairs, staying in the shadows. The next time Lisette came close to Caroline, he would be able to pounce and catch her.

"Start from the beginning," the other woman said. "And if you tell the truth, maybe I'll kill your boyfriend quickly and you won't have to watch him suffer."

Caroline looked into the video camera Lisette had set up on a tripod a few feet in front of her. "My name is Caroline Gill. I am here to set the record straight about Dr. Paul Trumpold and my claim that he attacked me."

Zane could tell getting the words out were difficult for Caroline. She was doing her best just to keep it together.

"I need some water, Lisette. I can't get through this

whole thing with my throat this dry. I was working at a fire all day today."

"Fine." Lisette did something to the camera, then stormed into the kitchen. When Zane heard the sink faucet come on, he stuck his hand over the banister.

"Caro," he whispered.

She looked up, eyes wide. He put his finger over his lips. "Anybody else here?" he asked as quietly as he could.

"No, just her." He could tell she wanted to say more, but there wasn't time.

"I'll jump her when she gives you the water."

He'd barely moved back into the shadows before Lisette came out of the kitchen. "You know, it's good that we stopped. It reminded me you can't be tied up when you give your confession. Then everyone is just going to think you were coerced."

Zane cursed under his breath as she picked up a knife and the gun again. She held the gun to Caroline's head once more as she cut the binds on her wrist. Zane couldn't risk the jump. She cut the rope on the other wrist before handing Caroline the water.

"Now, let's try this again. Take two." Lisette laughed wildly, like some demented film director.

They needed to get Lisette to come back over to the stairs but without the gun. Zane didn't know how to get her to do that without risking Caroline's life.

Caroline started talking again.

"My name is Caroline Gill. I'm here to set the record straight about my claim that Dr. Paul Trumpold attacked me."

Lisette's eyes narrowed as she paused the camera again. "I will come over there and cut you if you don't give me the truth."

"Okay, Lisette, the truth. You deserve that."

"Damn straight I do."

"Here's the truth." Caroline paused and took a deep breath. "I was standing right about here when someone knocked on my door. Do you know that hearing someone knock on a door still has the power to make me cower on the inside? Because right after I opened the door, your brother burst in, his fist striking my face before I could even react."

"Tell the truth, you bitch!" Lisette screeched.

"I am telling the truth. He hit me so hard that the bones in my cheek shattered. I fell to the floor, ironically, right here. Right here under my feet was where your brother attacked and raped me, Lisette."

Lisette stormed at Caroline, knife in hand. But a knife wasn't a gun and Zane was faster. He leaped over the banister, placing himself between Caroline and the madwoman rushing toward her. Lisette obviously wasn't expecting that. She brought the gun in her other hand up, but it was too late. With one quick uppercut Zane had the woman laid out on the floor.

He quickly took both weapons from her. She was already regaining consciousness and moaning as Zane handcuffed her hands behind her back.

"He hit me just like that, Lisette, but your brother didn't stop with just one punch," Caroline said hoarsely.

Then she sat down on the ground, on the floor where so much pain and humiliation had happened to her, and cried.

Chapter Twenty-Two

It was a beautiful day for a wedding.

Caroline had known Sherry Mitchell since they were both in college. They'd remained close through the years. Standing up here as part of the bridal party was an honor. She was delighted to be a part of her friend's special day.

A couple of weeks ago Caroline might have been nervous about standing in front of a hundred people. In a dress. In heels. None of those were things she was comfortable with. But given everything that had happened over the last two weeks, standing here didn't seem like such a terrorizing event after all.

Besides, she knew she looked good in the dress, especially if the way Zane couldn't take his eyes off her was anything to go by.

Maybe she'd have to start wearing dresses more often. Her paramedic uniform involved blue cargo pants and a blue button-down shirt. When she wasn't in that, she tended to be in jeans and a T-shirt.

No one would ever accuse Caroline of being too girlie.

But Zane hadn't taken his eyes off her from where he sat in the second row since the moment she'd walked down the aisle in front of Sherry a few minutes ago. He was still staring. And damn if she didn't like that hungry look in his eyes.

It was definitely enough to make a girl wear a dress more often.

Jon and Sherry had decided on a small wedding in a simple church just outside of Colorado Springs. Even being small there were nearly a hundred people here, many of them Omega Sector agents who worked with Jon and Sherry. They were more than just colleagues; it was easy to tell. They were family.

The wedding official was starting the charge to the bride and groom when Caroline caught sight of the videographer making his way straight up the middle aisle. The photographer had taken a much more conservative post in the back of the church.

Caroline tried to ignore the videographer, with the camera stuck to his face, but the guy seemed to be coming straight toward her, not caring at all about the service.

When she got married, she didn't want any disruptions like this guy. She would make sure that the videographer and photographer both knew she and Zane wouldn't tolerate a disruption like this.

Caroline's eyes flew to Zane's. Had she just made

wedding plans with him in her mind? She ought to wait until he actually asked her.

The videographer looked like he was going to come all the way up onto the platform with the minister. Caroline just rolled her eyes as he did exactly that. But instead of having his camera pointed at the bride and groom, it was pointed at her. And then he dropped it from the front of his face.

Caroline felt terror shoot through her.

It was Paul Trumpold. And he was coming toward her, gun now in hand.

She forced herself not to let the panic take her under. She needed her wits about her. No, this wasn't Paul Trumpold. He was dead.

But it was the man who had been in the doorway at the safe house and who she saw before the drugs had knocked her unconscious at the oil fire.

"That's right," he said. "I'm Nicholas. Paul and Lisette's brother."

How many violently crazy people could one family have?

She heard gasps and movements as Nicholas pulled her down in front of him, using her as a shield as he pointed his gun toward her head.

"You lied about my sister and my brother. He's dead and she's in jail because of you."

His voice, so similar to the one she heard in her nightmares, brought waves of terror. But this time she refused to give in.

She'd frozen the last time a man had grabbed her.

Forgotten all her training and panicked. She wouldn't let that happen again.

Nicholas obviously wasn't expecting any fight out of Caroline. She certainly hadn't given one as he'd watched Brodey try to take her from the safe house.

This idiot probably didn't know that he'd walked into a church full of highly trained special agents. Caroline didn't know if any of them were carrying weapons, but she knew Zane was. He'd balked about having to get a special permit for his ankle holster for the plane ride here yesterday. But he wasn't planning on going anywhere without a weapon after what had happened recently.

All she had to do was give Zane a chance and not let this guy drag her out of the building.

Caroline met eyes with Zane, who gave her the slightest nod. He knew what she was planning, in sync with her the way they always had been. He trusted her to be able to do it.

Without warning she let all her weight go limp in Trumpold's grasp around her throat. When he shifted his stance to get a better hold on her, she made her move. She threw her heeled shoe back as hard as she could, gouging him in the shin, causing him to loosen his hold. She spun in his loosened grip, bringing her elbow around to clock him in the jaw.

When his head snapped around at her strike, she continued her momentum, swinging her arms around in a double fist, knocking the gun out of his hand and straight toward Zane. Then Caroline dropped to the ground, out of the way.

She hadn't been there the day Zane shot Paul Trumpold, saving Jon's and Sherry's lives and ending Trumpold's reign of terror over so many women.

But she was here this time when he put a bullet in Trumpold's chest before he could get his gun up and pointed at her. She was sure it was just as impressive.

That was *her* man. And she loved him.

In the aftermath of the situation, it was easy to tell who was an Omega Sector agent and who wasn't.

Everybody from Omega came forward to make sure Nicholas Trumpold was secure. Everybody who wasn't an agent made a mad rush to an exit to get away from a possibly dangerous situation.

Knowing Trumpold was taken care of, Zane moved quickly to Caroline, his face worried. His hands were gentle, ready to pull away if she seemed overwhelmed by what had happened.

"Caro, are you okay?"

Was she okay? Was he kidding? She knew she was grinning like an idiot but couldn't find it in her to care.

She had not been another damn victim.

"Did you see that move? Would've been a hell of a lot easier if I hadn't been in this dress."

The worry slid out of his eyes and he pulled Caroline against his chest. "It was pretty impressive. Trumpold definitely didn't expect it."

"But you did. You knew I could do it."

He kissed her forehead. "Of course you could do it. You just had to believe in yourself."

He wrapped his arms tighter around her as a couple of agents handcuffed Trumpold.

"I guess he's not dead."

Steve Drackett, head of the Critical Response Division of Omega, shook his head. "No. He'll soon be joining his sister in prison. Charged with attempted murder and ruining a perfectly good wedding day."

They all looked up at the bride and groom. Sherry looked white as a ghost and Jon was holding her tightly.

"I'm so sorry, Sherry." Caroline left Zane's arms and walked toward her friend. "He ruined your wedding."

"No, that's not it," Sherry said, looking at Caroline, then over at Steve and the other Omega agents. "I saw Damien Freihof. He was in the back corner of the church." She pointed in the direction. "He gave me a wave, then left in the middle of the panic."

Zane could hear the muttered curses of the agents around him, toned down because they were in a church.

"How did he know about this wedding?" Steve asked. "How did either of them know about this?"

The wedding hadn't been a secret, but it hadn't been made public in any way, either. Omega had too many enemies for that, Freihof being number one of them.

"We've got a mole, Steve," Jon said. "We can't

deny that anymore. Damien is working with someone inside Omega Sector."

THE WEDDING WAS moved to the Omega Sector chow
hall. It was the only place big enough to hold all one
hundred guests.

And after what had happened, nobody minded
having to go through a metal detector to get to the
ceremony.

Jon and Sherry were determined that their wedding would go on. Today. Exactly one year to the day
from when Jon had proposed. Damien Freihof would
not stop them from getting married on the day they
had planned.

Zane had to admit it was the most unique wedding
he'd seen, but that didn't make it any less beautiful.
Maybe it was because the bride and groom were so
obviously in love with each other.

The caterers had transported the food over from
the original reception site, and the musicians had just
packed up their instruments and brought them over.
The cafeteria opened into a small terrace, so people
flowed both inside and out.

After the ceremony Zane planted an arm around
Caroline and didn't plan to let her go from his side
for the rest of the night.

Hell, he didn't know if he was going to let her go
from his side for the rest of forever.

"That was some pretty impressive teamwork you
two showed at the church today," Steve Drackett said

as they mulled around talking to people and eating the finger food.

"Thank you," Caroline said. "Although, we didn't plan it, believe me. I'm just glad I didn't freeze up."

"Well, if you two decide you're ready to get out of Corpus Christi, be sure to come see me about openings here at Omega. We could always use people who stay cool under pressure." Steve turned to Caroline. "And we could use a good medic for our SWAT team."

Zane loved Caroline's smile, and if she had expressed an interest in Steve's offer, Zane would've followed her lead.

"Sorry, afraid we're Texas folk, through and through. I don't think we could ever truly leave," Caroline said.

"I certainly respect that. But let me know if you change your mind."

A beautiful lady with a dark-haired baby in her arms came up to Steve. "No shoptalk at the wedding. I could tell from across the room you were talking business."

Steve reached down and kissed her and took the baby from her arms. "Busted." He smiled at Caroline and Zane as he led his wife back to the action.

Caroline turned to him, worry in her eyes. "I shouldn't have spoken for you, Zane. I'm sorry. Omega Sector might be a dream come true for you."

He wrapped his arms around her and pulled her closer. "No, I don't want to leave Texas. Especially not now just as I'm getting re-situated in the police department. Tim Harris would have my ass if I quit now, even for Omega Sector."

"You're really going to go back to the department full-time?"

"Yeah. It's where I belong. We both know that."

Her smile beamed. "Stay right here. I brought something with me and I think it's just about time."

"What is it?"

"I'll get it and show you."

"Maybe I don't want to let you go."

"I'm just going across the room." She rolled her eyes.

He pulled her up tight against him. "Maybe I'm not just talking about here. Maybe I'm talking about forever."

She reached up and put both her hands on his cheeks. "I can't promise you forever, Zane. Not yet. There's something missing."

He fought to tamp down the disappointment that swamped him at her words. She needed more time, he had to understand that. After what she'd been through, who could blame her for needing more time?

It was hard, but he let her go. He watched as she scurried across the room to a gift bag she'd brought and left by one of the doors. She'd had it on the plane and even had it at the church earlier. He'd assumed it was a gift for Jon and Sherry, but now she was bringing it back to him.

She held the string of the bag with one hand as she

stopped directly in front of him. She reached into it and pulled out his white cowboy hat.

Zane didn't know what to say. She must have grabbed it from his house, although he hadn't seen her do it. Before he could think of anything, she slipped it onto his head.

"Now," she whispered, dropping the bag and smiling up at him.

"Now what?" he said, unable to stop the smile spreading all over his face. He pulled her to him, knowing he would never be able to let her go again.

"Now you're ready to rejoin the force, and you and I are ready for our forever."

* * * * *

Look for the next book in Janie Crouch's
OMEGA SECTOR: UNDER SIEGE
miniseries next year.

And don't miss the previous title in the
OMEGA SECTOR: UNDER SIEGE *series:*

DADDY DEFENDER

Available now from Harlequin Intrigue!

Sheriff Flint Cahill can and will endure elements far worse than the coming winter storm to hunt down Maggie Thompson and her abductor.

Read on for a sneak preview of
COWBOY'S LEGACY,
A CAHILL RANCH NOVEL *from*
New York Times *bestselling author*
B.J. Daniels!

SHE WAS IN so fast that she didn't have a chance to scream. The icy cold water stole her breath away. Her eyes flew open as she hit. Because of the way she fell, she had no sense of up or down for a few moments.

Panicked, she flailed in the water until a light flickered above her. She tried to swim toward it, but something was holding her down. The harder she fought, the more it seemed to push her deeper and deeper, the light fading.

Her lungs burned. She had to breathe. The dim light wavered above her through the rippling water. She clawed at it as her breath gave out. She could see the surface just inches above her. Air! She needed oxygen. Now!

The rippling water distorted the face that suddenly appeared above her. The mouth twisted in a grotesque smile. She screamed, only to have her throat fill with the putrid dark water. She choked, sucking in even more water. She was drowning, and the person who'd done this to her was watching her die and smiling.

Maggie Thompson shot upright in bed, gasping for air and swinging her arms frantically toward the faint light coming through the window. Panic had her perspiration-soaked nightgown sticking to her skin. Trembling, she clutched the bedcovers as she gasped for breath.

The nightmare had been so real this time that she thought she was going to drown before she could come out of it. Her chest ached, her throat feeling raw as tears burned her eyes. It had been too real. She couldn't shake the feeling that she'd almost died this time. Next time…

She snapped on the bedside lamp to chase away the dark shadows hunkered in the corners of the room. If only Flint had been here instead of on an all-night stakeout. She needed Sheriff Flint Cahill's strong arms around her. Not that he stayed most nights. They hadn't been intimate that long.

Often, he had to work or was called out in the middle of the night. He'd asked her to move in with him months ago, but she'd declined. He'd asked her after one of his ex-wife's nasty tricks. Maggie hadn't wanted to make a decision like that based on Flint's ex.

While his ex hadn't done anything in months to keep them apart, Maggie couldn't rest easy. Flint was hoping Celeste had grown tired of her tricks. Maggie wasn't that naive. Celeste Duma was one of those women who played on every man's weakness to get what she wanted—and she wanted not just the rich, powerful man she'd left Flint for. She wanted to keep her ex on the string, as well.

Maggie's breathing slowed a little. She pulled the covers up to her chin, still shivering, but she didn't turn off the light. Sleep was out of the question for a while. She told herself that she wasn't going to let Celeste scare her. She wasn't going to give the woman the satisfaction.

Unfortunately, it was just bravado. Flint's ex was obsessed with him. Obsessed with keeping them apart. And since the woman had nothing else to do...

As the images of the nightmare faded, she reminded herself that the dream made no sense. It never had. She was a good swimmer. Loved water. Had never nearly drowned. Nor had anyone ever tried to drown her.

Shuddering, she thought of the face she'd seen through the rippling water. Not Celeste's. More like a Halloween mask. A distorted smiling face, neither male nor female. Just the memory sent her heart racing again.

What bothered her most was that dream kept reoccurring. After the first time, she'd mentioned it to her friend Belle Delaney.

"A drowning dream?" Belle had asked with the arch of her eyebrow. "Do you feel that in waking life you're being 'sucked into' something you'd rather not be a part of?"

Maggie had groaned inwardly. Belle had never kept it a secret that she thought Maggie was making a mistake when it came to Flint. Too much baggage, she always said of the sheriff. His "baggage" came in the shape of his spoiled, probably psychopathic, petite, green-eyed, blonde ex.

"I have my own skeletons." Maggie had laughed, although she'd never shared her past—even with Belle—before moving to Gilt Edge, Montana, and opening her beauty shop, Just Hair. She feared it was her own baggage that scared her the most.

"If you're holding anything back," Belle had said, eyeing her closely, "you need to let it out. Men hate surprises after they tie the knot."

"Guess I don't have to worry about that because Flint hasn't said anything about marriage." But she knew Belle was right. She'd even come close to telling him several times about her past. Something had always stopped her. The truth was, she feared if he found out her reasons for coming to Gilt Edge he wouldn't want her anymore.

"The dream isn't about Flint," she'd argued that day with Belle, but she couldn't shake the feeling that it was a warning.

"Well, from what I know about dreams," Belle had said, "if in the dream you survive the drowning, it means that a waking relationship will ultimately survive the turmoil. At least, that is one interpretation. But I'd say the nightmare definitely indicates that you are going into unknown waters and something is making you leery of where you're headed." She'd cocked an eyebrow at her. "If you have the dream again, I'd suggest that you ask yourself what it is you're so afraid of."

"I'm sure it's just about his ex, Celeste," she'd lied. Or was she afraid that she wasn't good enough for Flint—just as his ex had warned her. Just as she feared in her heart.

THE WIND LAY over the tall dried grass and kicked up dust as Sheriff Flint Cahill stood on the hillside. He shoved his Stetson down on his head of thick dark hair, squinting in the distance at the clouds to the west. Sure as the devil, it was going to snow before the day was out.

In the distance, he could see a large star made out of red and green lights on the side of a barn, a reminder that Christmas was coming. Flint thought he might even get a tree this year, go up in the mountains and cut it himself. He hadn't had a tree at Christmas in years. Not since...

At the sound of a pickup horn, he turned, shielding his eyes from the low winter sun. He could smell snow in the air, feel it deep in his bones. This storm was going to dump a good foot on them, according to the latest news. They were going to have a white Christmas.

Most years he wasn't ready for the holiday season any more than he was ready for a snow that wouldn't melt until spring. But this year was different. He felt energized. This was the year his life would change. He thought of the small velvet box in his jacket pocket. He'd been carrying it around for months. Just the thought of it made him smile to himself. He was in love and he was finally going to do something about it.

The pickup rumbled to a stop a few yards from him. He took a deep breath of the mountain air and, telling himself he was ready for whatever Mother Nature wanted to throw at him, he headed for the truck.

"Are you all right?" his sister asked as he slid into the passenger seat. In the cab out of the wind, it was nice and warm. He rubbed his bare hands together, wishing he hadn't forgotten his gloves earlier. But when he'd headed out, he'd had too much on his mind. He still did.

Lillie looked out at the dull brown of the landscape and the chain-link fence that surrounded the missile silo. "What were you doing out here?"

He chuckled. "Looking for aliens. What else?" This was the spot that their father swore aliens hadn't just landed on one night back in 1967. Nope, according to Ely Cahill, the aliens had abducted him, taken him aboard their spaceship and done experiments on him. Not that anyone believed it in the county. Everyone just assumed that Ely had a screw loose. Or two.

It didn't help that their father spent most of the year up in the mountains as a recluse trapping and panning for gold.

"Aliens. Funny," Lillie said, making a face at him.

He smiled over at her. "Actually, I was on an all-night stakeout. The cattle rustlers didn't show up." He shrugged.

She glanced around. "Where's your patrol SUV?"

"Axle deep in a muddy creek back toward Grass Range. I'll have to get it pulled out. After I called you, I started walking and I ended up here. Wish I'd grabbed my gloves, though."

"You're scaring me," she said, studying him openly. "You're starting to act like Dad."

He laughed at that, wondering how far from the truth it was. "At least I didn't see any aliens near the missile silo."

She groaned. Being the butt of jokes in the county because of their father got old for all of them.

Flint glanced at the fenced-in area. There was nothing visible behind the chain link but tumbleweeds. He turned back to her. "I didn't pull you away from anything important, I hope? Since you were close by, I thought you wouldn't mind giving me a ride. I've had enough walking for one day. Or thinking, for that matter."

She shook her head. "What's going on, Flint?"

He looked out at the country that ran to the mountains. Cahill Ranch. His grandfather had started it, his father had worked it and now two of his brothers ran the cattle part of it to keep the place going while he and his sister, Lillie, and brother Darby had taken other paths. Not to mention their oldest brother, Tucker, who'd struck out at seventeen and hadn't been seen or heard from since.

Flint had been scared after his marriage and divorce. But Maggie was nothing like Celeste, who was small, blonde, green-eyed and crazy. Maggie was tall with big brown eyes and long auburn hair. His heart beat faster at the thought of her smile, at her laugh.

"I'm going to ask Maggie to marry me," Flint said and nodded as if reassuring himself.

When Lillie didn't reply, he glanced over at her. It wasn't like her not to have something to say. "Well?"

"What has taken you so long?"

He sighed. "Well, you know after Celeste…"

"Say no more," his sister said, raising a hand to stop him. "Anyone would be gun-shy after being married to her."

"I'm hoping she won't be a problem."

Lillie laughed. "Short of killing your ex-wife, she is always going to be a problem. You just have to decide if you're going to let her run your life. Or if you're going to live it—in spite of her."

So easy for her to say. He smiled, though. "You're right. Anyway, Maggie and I have been dating for a while now and there haven't been any…incidents in months."

Lillie shook her head. "You know Celeste was the one who vandalized Maggie's beauty shop—just as you know she started that fire at Maggie's house."

"Too bad there wasn't any proof so I could have arrested her. But since there wasn't and no one was hurt and it was months ago…"

"I'd love to see Celeste behind bars, though I think

prison is too good for her. I can understand why you would be worried about what she will do next. She's psychopathic."

He feared that that maybe was close to the case. "Do you want to see the ring?" He knew she did, so he fished it out of his pocket. He'd been carrying it around for quite a while now. Getting up his courage? He knew what was holding him back. Celeste. He couldn't be sure how she would take it—or what she might do. His ex-wife seemed determined that he and Maggie shouldn't be together, even though she was apparently happily married to local wealthy businessman Wayne Duma.

Handing his sister the small black velvet box, he waited as she slowly opened it.

A small gasp escaped her lips. "It's beautiful. *Really* beautiful." She shot him a look. "I thought sheriffs didn't make much money?"

"I've been saving for a long while now. Unlike my sister, I live pretty simply."

She laughed. "Simply? Prisoners have more in their cells than you do. You aren't thinking of living in that small house of yours after you're married, are you?"

"For a while. It's not that bad. Not all of us have huge new houses like you and Trask."

"We need the room for all the kids we're going to have," she said. "But it is wonderful, isn't it? Trask is determined that I have everything I ever wanted."

Her gaze softened as the newlywed thought of her husband.

"I keep thinking of your wedding." There'd been a double wedding, with both Lillie and her twin, Darby, getting married to the loves of their lives only months ago. "It's great to see you and Trask so happy. And Darby and Mariah... I don't think Darby is ever going to come off that cloud he's on."

Lillie smiled. "I'm so happy for him. And I'm happy for you. You know I really like Maggie. So do it. Don't worry about Celeste. Once you're married, there's nothing she can do."

He told himself she was right, and yet in the back of his mind, he feared that his ex-wife would do something to ruin it—just as she had done to some of his dates with Maggie.

"I don't understand Celeste," Lillie was saying as she shifted into Drive and started toward the small Western town of Gilt Edge. "She's the one who dumped you for Wayne Duma. So what is her problem?"

"I'm worried that she is having second thoughts about her marriage to Duma. Or maybe she's bored and has nothing better to do than concern herself with my life. Maybe she just doesn't want me to be happy."

"Or she is just plain malicious," Lillie said. "If she isn't happy, she doesn't want you to be, either."

A shaft of sunlight came through the cab window, warming him against the chill that came with even talking about Celeste. He leaned back, content as Lillie drove.

He was going to ask Maggie to marry him. He was going to do it this weekend. He'd already made a dinner reservation at the local steak house. He had the ring in his pocket. Now it was just a matter of popping the question and hoping she said yes. If she did… Well, then, this was going to be the best Christmas ever, he thought and smiled.

* * * * *

Don't miss COWBOY'S LEGACY,
available December 2017
wherever HQN Books and
ebooks are sold.

www.Harlequin.com

INTRIGUE

Available December 19, 2017

#1755 GUNFIRE ON THE RANCH
Blue River Ranch • by Delores Fossen

DEA agent Theo Carter was a suspect in his parents' murder...and now he's back to protect the family he never knew he had.

#1756 SAFE AT HAWK'S LANDING
Badge of Justice • by Rita Herron

Charlotte Reacher is no stranger to the trauma her students have experienced, and as she's the only witness to a human-trafficking abduction, FBI agent Lucas Hawk will have his work cut out for him keeping her safe.

#1757 WHISPERING SPRINGS
by Amanda Stevens

This high school reunion was a shot at redemption and maybe a second chance for former army ranger Dylan Burkhart and his old flame Ava North. But a secret-telling game turns up a murder confession, with the killer hiding among them...

#1758 RANGER PROTECTOR
Texas Brothers of Company B • by Angi Morgan

After Megan Harper is framed for a fatal shooting, protecting her becomes Texas Ranger Jack McKinnon's sole mission...until unspoken desire gets in the way.

#1759 SOLDIER'S PROMISE
The Ranger Brigade: Family Secrets • by Cindi Myers

Different circumstances brought officer Jake Lohmiller and undercover Ranger Brigade sergeant Carmen Redhorse to a cult encampment in Colorado, but teaming up might be their only shot at saving their families... and each other.

#1760 FORGOTTEN PIECES
The Protectors of Riker County • by Tyler Anne Snell

To say Riker County detective Matt Walker and journalist Maggie Carson have bad blood is an understatement. But when the last twenty-four hours of her memory go missing and she gets caught in someone's crosshairs, the lawman who hates her may be her only salvation...

YOU CAN FIND MORE INFORMATION ON UPCOMING HARLEQUIN® TITLES, FREE EXCERPTS AND MORE AT WWW.HARLEQUIN.COM.

HICNM1217

Get 2 Free Books,

HARLEQUIN

INTRIGUE

Plus 2 Free Gifts—

just for trying the Reader Service!

HI17R2

SPECIAL EXCERPT FROM

HHARLEQUIN®

I N T R I G U E

*To say Riker County detective Matt Walker and
journalist Maggie Carson have bad blood is an
understatement. But when the last twenty-four hours
of her memory go missing and she gets caught in
someone's crosshairs, the lawman who hates her may be
her only salvation...*

Read on for a sneak preview of
FORGOTTEN PIECES
by Tyler Anne Snell.

Everyone worked through grief differently.

Some people started a new hobby; some people threw themselves into the gym.

Others investigated unsolved murders in secret.

"And why, of all people, would you need me here?" Matt asked, cutting through her mental breakdown of him.

Instead of stepping backward, utilizing the large open space of her front porch, she chanced a step forward.

"I found something," she started, straining out any excess enthusiasm that might make her seem coarse. Still, she knew the detective was a keen observer. Which was why his frown was already doubling in on itself before she explained herself.

"I don't want to hear this," he interrupted, his voice like ice. "I'm warning you, Carson."

"And it wouldn't be the first time you've done so," she countered, skipping over the fact he'd said her last name like a teacher getting ready to send her to detention. "But right now I'm telling you I found a lead. A real, honest-to-God lead!"

The detective's frown affected all of his body. It pinched his expression and pulled his posture taut. Through gritted teeth, he rumbled out his thoughts with disdain clear in his words.

"Why do you keep doing this? What gives you the right?" He took a step away from her. That didn't stop Maggie.

"It wasn't an accident," she implored. "I can prove it now."

Matt shook his head. He skipped frustrated and flew right into angry. This time Maggie faltered.

"You have no right digging into this," he growled. "You didn't even know Erin."

"But don't you want to hear what I found?"

Matt made a stop motion with his hands. The jaw she'd been admiring was set. Hard. "I don't want to ever talk to you again. Especially about this." He turned and was off the front porch in one fluid motion. Before he got into his truck he paused. "And next time you call me out here, I won't hesitate to arrest you."

And then he was gone.

Don't miss
FORGOTTEN PIECES
available January 2018 wherever
Harlequin® Intrigue books and ebooks are sold.

www.Harlequin.com

HIEXP1217

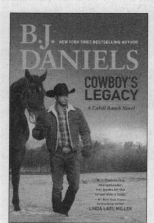

$7.99 U.S./$9.99 CAN.

EXCLUSIVE
Limited Time Offer

$1.⁰⁰ OFF

New York Times bestselling author
B.J. DANIELS
returns to her captivating *Cahill Ranch*
series with a brand-new tale!

COWBOY'S LEGACY

Available November 28, 2017.
Pick up your copy today!

HQN™

$1.⁰⁰ OFF
the purchase price of
COWBOY'S LEGACY by B.J. Daniels.

Offer valid from November 28, 2017, to December 31, 2017.
Redeemable at participating retail outlets. Not redeemable at Barnes & Noble.
Limit one coupon per purchase. Valid in the U.S.A. and Canada only.

52615069

5 65373 00076 2   (8100)0 12302

® and ™ are trademarks owned and used by the trademark owner and/or its licensee.

© 2017 Harlequin Enterprises Limited

PHCOUPBJDHI1217